REVENGE OF THE ENGINERDS

The first epic adventure:

EngiNerds

REVENGE OF THE ENGINERDS

JARRETT LERNER

PARP!

Aladdin

NEW YORK LONDON TORONTO
SYDNEY NEW DELHI

ALADDIN

An imprint of Simon & Schuster Children's Publishing Division
1230 Avenue of the Americas, New York, New York 10020
First Aladdin hardcover edition February 2019
Text copyright © 2019 by Jarrett Lerner
Jacket and interior illustrations copyright © 2019 by Serge Seidlitz
All rights reserved, including the right of reproduction in whole or in part in any form.
ALADDIN and related logo are registered trademarks of Simon & Schuster, Inc.
For information about special discounts for bulk purchases,
please contact Simon & Schuster Special Sales at 1-866-506-1949
or business@simonandschuster.com.
The Simon & Schuster Speakers Bureau can bring authors to your live event. For more information or to book an event contact the Simon & Schuster Speakers Bureau at 1-866-248-3049 or visit our website at www.simonspeakers.com.
Jacket designed by Karin Paprocki
Interior designed by Hilary Zarycky
The text of this book was set in Amasis.
Manufactured in the United States of America 0119 FFG
2 4 6 8 10 9 7 5 3 1
Library of Congress Control Number 2018959532
ISBN 978-1-4814-6874-9 (hc)
ISBN 978-1-4814-6876-3 (eBook)

For Isla

Preface

SATURDAY NIGHT, THERE WAS THE BLACKOUT.
For two hours our entire town was inexplicably without power.

Then, the very next morning, the satellite—it just came plummeting out of the sky.

And yesterday—Monday—we woke up to the news about the Food-Plus. That's this little grocery store people go to when they can't make it over to the Shop & Save.

But no one's going to be shopping *there* any time soon. The whole place—every last stick of gum and bite-size mini muffin—was mysteriously cleaned out overnight. There wasn't a single crumb of food left on the shelves.

Do I know for a fact that all this mischief was caused by the endlessly hungry, dangerously flatulent robot currently on the loose?

No, I don't.

But who *else* could be doing it?

The robot is on the loose thanks to Mike Edsley, the stupidest genius you'll ever meet. The kid dismantled, repaired, and rebuilt the engine of his neighbor's busted lawnmower at the age of six. But put him in a situation that requires the use of even the slightest bit of common sense, and Edsley will disappoint you every time.

It was my best friend, Dan, who built the robots.

Eighteen of them.

Yep—you read that right.

One-eight.

The robots were programmed to cram their stomachs full of food (or "comestibles," as they liked to call it), squash it all down into these tiny cubes, and store the cubes in their stomachs until their human owners got hungry. The robots were *not* supposed to endanger the lives of their human owners by firing those food-cubes out of their backsides at around ninety miles per hour. But they did, and—

Well, if you want to know what happened next, there's a whole book about it.

All you really need to know is that, with a little help from a spontaneous rainstorm, we did away with sixteen of the bots—*we* being me, Dan, and our friends

Jerry and John Henry Knox. The seventeenth bot was never assembled. Figuring the world didn't need any more of these butt-blasters among its population, we split up that bot's parts into four piles, then packed each pile into a box. I've got a box, and so do Dan and Jerry and John Henry Knox. Mine's under my bed, cinched shut with about thirty yards of duct tape.

Which brings us back to last bot, Number Eighteen, who's out there on the loose because Edsley—that brilliant, brilliant idiot—refused to make him a sandwich. A *second* sandwich, to be precise, right after the guy had stuck the first one into his big metal belly. Edsley's refusal sparked a heated argument, which ended with the robot attempting to tear off the kid's face with a razor-sharp claw, all before stomping out of the house, down the street, and out of sight.

Edsley, being Edsley, just let him go.

And so here we are.

Satellites are falling out of the sky.

Grocery stores are getting cleaned out.

And it's up to us, the EngiNerds, to find the robot and put a stop to him before things can get even worse.

If, that is, I can get any of the other guys to actually help me. . . .

THREE DAYS.

That's how long we've been looking for Edsley's robot.

Maybe that doesn't seem like that much time to you.

But each of those days contained twenty-four long hours.

That's seventy-two hours—or *4,320 minutes*—for that hungry, hungry robot to cause as much chaos, mayhem, and destruction as he pleased.

Over the course of those nearly forty-five hundred minutes, we've tried nearly everything to find the bot.

Some of our plans have been good. Some of them have been not-so-good. And a few, unfortunately, have been downright ridiculous.

And let me tell you—it hasn't been easy to keep the morale up and the momentum going among the guys. They went from determined to discouraged in about a day and a half, and now the majority of them are something even worse: distracted.

All of which has left me feeling desperate.

That's why I'm currently at the park with Edsley, twenty-six rotisserie chickens, and a pair of giant, industrial-strength fans. A part of me already knows this plan is one of our *most* not-so-good ones. But at least I'm doing *something*. At least I'm actively trying to find the robot before he blasts someone with a turd-missile or, I don't know, finds his way onto a computer and breaks the Internet.

Dan had a dentist appointment right after school today, and Edsley was the only other one of the guys I could convince to come with me—and only because I've been hammering into him every chance I get that it's all his fault the robot is on the loose and we've been spending so much time and energy looking for the thing in the first place.

Also, I promised to let him eat some of the chicken.

I turn to him.

"Mike!" I shout. "I said *some*, not *all*."

He holds his hands up, professing his innocence. His fingers are slick with chicken grease.

I shake my head and sigh.

"Will you just plug the fans in, man?"

Edsley reaches for my portable power pack. I wince,

thinking about how nasty he's going to leave the handle. I make a mental note to wipe it down with some disinfectant when I get home, then get the fans into position.

Here's the plan:

Step one—aim one fan one way, aim the other fan the other way.

Step two—set up half the rotisserie chickens in front of each fan and then turn those bad boys on full blast, sending the smell of the warm, oven-baked birds wafting across town.

Step three—wait for the missing robot's scent sensors to pick up on the irresistible aroma and come find us.

When he does, Edsley and I will douse the guy in water.

And then?

SQUAH-POOM!

Problem solved.

Because if there's one thing I'm sure of, it's that this robot has spent the past three days stuffing his stomach full of food and then squashing down all his meals and snacks into ultra-compact food-cubes. And when those puppies touch water, they expand, and rapidly enough to rip Mr. Dis-POS-al COM-*pleeet* apart.

"Ready?" I ask Edsley.

He places the last chicken on one of the overturned trash barrels we've got set up in front of the fans, then gives me a thumbs-up.

"*Please work . . . ,*" I mutter to myself.

I flip the switch on the power pack and the fans whir to life.

2.

DO I REALLY NEED TO TELL YOU HOW THE chicken-and-fan plan turned out?

Let's just say that the only butt-blaster that got doused in water was Edsley, after he "accidentally" sent a gust of some particularly foul gas in my direction.

That was after an hour and a half of sitting at the park with him, listening to those fans whir and wondering how many washes it'd be before my clothes no longer reeked of chicken, all while baking like birds in an oven ourselves under the unseasonably hot mid-May sun. I gave it another thirty minutes, then slumped home in defeat.

At lunch the next day, I don't even bother giving the rest of the EngiNerds an update.

I just move on.

"So," I say, opening a notebook to a blank page as I make my way up to the front of the room, "how'd the brainstorming go last night? Let's hear some new ideas about how to find this bot."

Crickets.

The guys just blink up at me.

The ones who are even looking at me, that is.

Some are completely tuned out, doing their own thing.

And I get it.

I do.

They're sick of banging their heads against the same problem and not making any progress.

I'm frustrated too.

But I'm also scared. Scared of what might happen if the robot shows up in the wrong place at the wrong time. And scared of what might happen if, after such an unfortunate incident, the bot gets traced back to Dan. Because he could get in some serious trouble. Maybe even *jail*-like trouble.

All of a sudden Edsley leaps up onto his feet.

His eyes are wide.

His mouth is hanging open.

"I've got it," he gasps. "I figured it out. We don't need to look for the robot anymore."

3.

ALL EYES ARE ON EDSLEY.

"It's been *four* days now," he says.

"I'm aware," I tell him, trying to hurry him along.

He looks at me like I'm being dense.

"Don't you see?"

I shake my head, then check on the rest of the guys. They look just as confused as I am.

"The robot's batteries," Edsley says. "By now, they've *gotta* be dead."

My heart sinks, and my face must fall with it.

"What?" Edsley says.

"Dan," I ask, nice and slow for Edsley's benefit, "do the robots run on batteries?"

"They do not," Dan answers.

"Oh," Edsley says, sitting back down.

"*But . . .*"

It's Dan again.

"But *what?*" I ask him, careful not to let myself get *too* hopeful.

"I don't think it's outside the realm of possibility that the bot has taken itself out of commission."

I raise an eyebrow.

"Like maybe he fell in a ditch," Dan explains.

"That's what I was thinking!" says Max.

"Or he could've—"

"Slipped in a puddle!" Amir jumps in.

"Exactly," Dan says. "The bot might've done *something* to prevent him from eating and digesting and then, you know . . ."

"Shooting food-cubes out of his bum at *wicked* fast speeds?" Jerry says with a smile.

Dan doesn't smile back.

"Yeah . . . ," he says. "That."

"So I was right," Edsley says, leaping back up onto his feet. "We *can* stop looking for the robot."

The rest of the guys look relieved. They lean back in their chairs. They let their shoulders sag.

And I really hate to burst their bubble. But most of these guys didn't see the robots at their worst, when they were rampaging in back of the Shop & Save on

Saturday afternoon. Dan, Jerry, John Henry Knox, and I told them about it. Dozens of times. But it's just one of those things—you had to be there to really, truly *get* it.

So burst their bubble I must.

4.

"GUYS—*OF COURSE* WE CAN'T STOP LOOKING for the bot."

Shoulders stiffen.

Expressions turn glum.

"Maybe the thing *is* in a ditch," I go on. "But what if he *gets up*? These things are sophisticated, remember? They can *learn*. And the longer the bot's out there, the more he's learning."

Thinking about what terrifying new skills the missing bot might've mastered makes my skin crawl.

I shove the thought out of my head as Edsley raises his hand.

"Do I even want to know?" I ask him.

"What if it's a *really deep* ditch?" he says.

I don't answer, but just turn back to the rest of the guys.

"Think about it," I tell them. "Even if the robot fell into a"—I glance at Edsley—"*really deep ditch*, wouldn't we have come across it by now? We've spent the past four days trudging back and forth all over town. And Dan, you said the bot couldn't have made it more than five miles from Edsley's place, right?"

"Five miles *tops*," says Dan. "They're programmed not to wander too far from their home base."

"Okay," I say. "So how about this?" I hold up the notebook I brought to the front of the room with me. "Let's make a list of all the places this food-obsessed bot could be within a five-mile radius of Edsley's house. Anywhere that's got a *lot* of food—let's write it down. Even if we've already looked there, we'll look again. And along the way, we'll check every ditch and puddle we see. If we're logical about this, if we're methodical, we'll find the robot. We *have* to."

I grab my pencil.

"I'll start," I say, scribbling something down in my notebook.

"General Noodles," I share with the guys. "That's right around the corner from your place—isn't it, Edsley?"

He nods. Then says:

"So is Cheese Louise's."

"Perfect," I say, and add the name of the pizza shop to my list. "You guys got any more for me?"

"Mad Cow's," Dan says.

I add it.

Then he fires off a bunch more:

"The Eatery. Animal Chin's. Country Joe's. Cate's. That little breakfast place by the gas station."

"Good, good, good, good, good," I say. "Now we just need to spend this afternoon checking all these places out. We can look around for evidence, ask the employees if there've been any, you know, robot-related incidents. If we work together, we can put this whole mess to rest by the end of the day. So, who wants to go where?"

Silence.

"Guys," I say.

Then:

"Please?"

And finally, I get a response.

But it's not the one I'm looking for.

"Ahem."

It's John Henry Knox, clearing his throat and rising to his feet.

5.

JOHN HENRY KNOX MARCHES PAST ME AND
right up to the whiteboard. And as I watch him reach for
a marker, a part of me thinks that maybe the kid is actually about to be helpful, that he'll put his sizeable brain
to work improving upon my most-recent plan and help
me once and for all locate the missing bot.

But then I see what he's drawing.

Clouds.

"No," I say.

John Henry Knox doesn't hear me. Or he probably
does hear me, but just chooses to ignore me.

"*Hey*," I say. "Cloudy McCloudface."

That gets him.

He pulls his marker away from the board and turns
to face me, sighing like somehow *I'm* the one being
ridiculous.

"Kennedy," he says, "are you familiar with Albert
Einstein's definition of insanity?"

I consider asking him if he's familiar with what it feels like to be hit in the face with a cinnamon-raisin bagel, because I'm about two seconds away from hurling my lunch at his head.

"Doing the same thing over and over again and expecting different results," John Henry Knox tells me. "*That* is the definition of insanity, according to one of human history's greatest minds."

"Are you saying *that's* what we've been doing these past few days?"

He widens his eyes meaningfully.

"Okay," I admit. "That's kind of what we've been doing."

I spin around to face the rest of the guys before I lose them.

"Listen," I say, "I know how you're all feeling. Believe me—I do. But we've *got* to see this thing through. We can't just leave the bot out there on the loose. I mean, guys—there are satellites *falling out of the sky*."

"Satel*lites*?" Simon says. "I thought it was just the one."

"Yeah, it was," I give him. "But *still*."

"And you really think that was because of the bot?" Jerry asks.

"Yes. No. I . . . I don't know."

I take a deep breath.

"All I know is that a lot of weird stuff has been happening around here lately. And when a lot of weird stuff happens all at once, in the same general area, I don't think it's a bad idea to look into whether all of it's connected somehow. This robot's been out there for four days now. That's a *long* time. We have no idea what it's been up to, what new things it's learned how to do."

Jerry's nodding.

So is Dan.

Then Alan is, and then so are Max and Amir.

Suddenly, a quote pops into my head. Not one from Albert Einstein, but from another of human history's greatest minds—my grandpa.

"Before he retired," I tell the guys, "my grandpa had this note card hanging up in his office. And do you know what it said on it?" I pause to give the moment some drama. "It said, 'Finish what you start, or down the road, it'll bite you in the backside.'"

This gets a couple more guys nodding.

And a second later, there are a couple more.

I'm about to get down to business, to start assigning each of the guys a different food place to check out that afternoon, when I'm interrupted by a *whoosh*.

It's the door, swinging open.

And standing there in the doorway is something maybe even more shocking than a walking, talking, butt-blasting bot.

It's a *girl*.

I KNOW THE GIRL.

Well, sort of.

I've seen her around, and I know that she's a little . . . *strange*.

Every day she wears a different T-shirt with something kooky on it. Sometimes it's a drawing of a little green bug-eyed alien. Other times it's a constellation map or a close-up, high-resolution photo of Jupiter or Saturn. And other times it's just a saying, printed in big, bold letters. I BELIEVE or THE TRUTH IS OUT THERE—weird stuff like that.

I wait for the girl to say something, to let us know what she's doing here in *our* room.

She doesn't.

She just looks around at each of the guys, inspecting them like she's sizing us all up for some sort of super-important mission.

"Can I *help* you?" I finally ask, making sure there's

enough sarcasm in my voice so she knows that I don't actually *want* to help her, that I just want her to hurry up and leave.

But apparently the girl doesn't *get* sarcasm.

She strides into the room like she owns the place, then plants herself right up front, next to me.

"I hope so," she says at last.

I give her my best *are you serious* glare.

Then I tell her, "Look. I don't know who you are—"

"Mikaela Harrington," she says.

"—or what you're doing here—"

"I came to talk about the extraterrestrial activity."

"—but . . ."

My sentence goes unfinished, and I'm left gaping at the girl for several seconds.

"What was that?" I eventually manage.

"The aliens," Mikaela says. "The ones in our town."

7.

ALIENS?

In *our* town?

This girl is even kookier than I thought.

"Are you telling me you haven't noticed?" she asks me.

Before I can answer, she turns to face the rest of the guys.

One by one, they all drop their eyes and start fidgeting with their notebooks and binders. That's because unless you count moms and sisters, the EngiNerds don't have much experience interacting with members of the opposite sex—especially not ones who waltz in on us totally unawares, oozing certainty and self-confidence.

"None of you?" Mikaela says.

"No," I tell her, bringing her attention back to me. "We haven't noticed any *aliens*."

Mikaela frowns.

"I thought you guys were nerds."

"Not *those* kind of nerds," I tell her. "We're into science. Not science *fiction*."

"This isn't fiction," Mikaela says. Then she starts slapping her fingers into her palm, listing off all of this supposed evidence of extraterrestrial activity. "First there was the blackout. Then there was the satellite. And after that the Food-Plus—the place got totally emptied out."

"Yeah," I say. "We know about all that. But none of it was caused by *aliens*."

Mikaela grins.

"Then what caused it?"

I open my mouth to answer.

But stop myself just in time.

Because I don't need to tell Mikaela about the missing bot.

All I need to tell her is that the rest of the guys and I are busy, and aren't interested in hearing about her silly ideas.

And I'm about to—but then I see that she's staring at something across the room, her eyes lit up like she just found what she came here looking for.

I follow her gaze . . .

. . . and find Dan.

8.

DAN AND MIKAELA LOCK EYES FOR WHAT

feels like an hour.

It just.

Doesn't.

End.

And I know what she's doing:

Daring him to ask her a question, to start a conversation about *extraterrestrial activity*.

I step between the two of them before he can get tricked into doing it.

"Look," I tell Mikaela, "we're busy. *Really* busy."

I motion toward the door, letting her know that it's time for her to use it and get lost.

She doesn't.

She narrows her eyes and looks at me long and hard. Then she nods, like something's just clicked in her head.

I don't think it's what I *want* to have click in there, though—that not a single one of us is interested in her aliens-in-our-town mumbo jumbo, and that she need not come back to bother us ever again.

But before I can do or say anything else to help get the message across, Mikaela finally does head for the door. She exits with the same self-assured stride she entered with, hooking her toe on the door's edge and swinging it shut behind her.

"What a weirdo," I say, chuckling as I turn back to the guys.

None of them laugh along with me.

"*What a weirdo*," I repeat a little more emphatically.

The guys smile and nod.

Except for Dan.

He's staring at the closed door.

His face is blank.

He's not even *blinking*.

But he must feel my eyes on him.

Because eventually he turns to me.

And at last he smiles.

It's small, though, and I can tell it's forced.

9.

AT THE END OF THE DAY, I ALMOST DON'T
even stop by my locker. Jerry's got a family thing he has
to go to, and John Henry Knox made it pretty clear at
lunch how he felt about my continuing to search for the
missing bot. I'm nervous none of the other guys will be
there waiting for me. Not even Dan. And that . . .

Well, I just don't know if I can take it.

But I go, refusing to believe the worst about my best
friend.

And Dan doesn't disappoint.

He's there, as is Edsley.

I could hug him.

Dan, obviously, not Mike—I wouldn't have really
minded if *he* didn't show.

We head to my house, since I need to walk my dog,
Kitty, before we get the robot hunt underway. But once
we get there, I think better of it and decide to just bring
the pooch along. I'm thinking he might be able to help

us. You know, put that powerful schnoz of his to work.

Big mistake.

"OW!" I shout as Kitty nearly tugs my arm right out of its socket.

He's been yanking me in random directions ever since we stepped outside. I've never seen him like this before. It's like he's possessed, and it's making it impossible to do any actual robot-hunting.

And Dan and Edsley?

They don't even seem to care.

Dan's got his head tipped back. He's staring up at the clouds in the sky like he's John Henry Knox Junior.

Edsley, meanwhile, has his hand in his armpit. He's flapping his elbow up and down like he's doing the chicken dance, his sweaty flesh producing a series of disgusting fartlike sounds.

I think back to just a few days ago. . . .

To my shattered kitchen window.

To the gaping holes in my bedroom wall.

To the Channel 5 News Team's *ROBOTS ATTACK* coverage.

To all the terrified people at the farmers' market and the bakery.

To me and Dan and Jerry and John Henry Knox in

the alleyway behind the Shop & Save, finally finding out just what these robots are capable of.

Edsley makes his armpit fart again.

He giggles.

And I snap.

"GUYS!"

Dan looks down.

Edsley pulls his arm out of his T-shirt.

I take a deep breath.

"Sorry," I say.

Because as frustrated as I am, I know we're not going to make any progress if we start fighting with one another.

"I'm just worried, all right? And feeling a little—OW!"

Kitty.

10.

WE DECIDE TO LET KITTY LEAD US AROUND

for a few minutes, hoping he'll tire himself out and then let *us* lead *him* around. You know, like how it usually works with people and their dogs.

Soon enough, though, it starts to look like Kitty has a specific destination in mind.

"I think he wants to go to Things & Stuff," Dan says, pointing to the store across the street that the dog is cutting off his air supply in a desperate attempt to reach.

Edsley wrinkles his nose.

"Ugh," he says.

And I can't help but agree.

Things & Stuff is this weird little store that seems to sell both everything and nothing. They've got motor oil and shoelaces and watering cans, but none of the stuff you might more regularly need—like, say, toilet paper or pens. The store is only open at bizarre, random hours, their prices are far from competitive, and the place is run by a guy named Stan who hates—and I mean *hates*—kids. If you're under the age of twenty-five and step into his establishment, he automatically assumes you're there to steal a pack of thumbtacks or burn the place to the ground. I have no clue how the place has stayed in business so long.

For all these reasons, I do my best to avoid Things & Stuff, just like every other kid (and the majority of adults) in town. But I brought Kitty there once when my mom sent me out to find one of those super tiny screwdrivers you use to fix eyeglasses, and back behind the store the dog found this big, nasty Dumpster, and in Kitty's world, a big, nasty Dumpster is like a treasure chest full of gold.

I tell the guys about the Dumpster.

"He found this dirty sock under there, and now it's, like, his all-time favorite dirty sock."

As if he can under-
stand what I'm saying,
Kitty strains against his
leash even more.

"Man," Edsley says.
"Must be some dirty
sock."

"It is," I tell him.

Dan scratches the back of his head.

"Hold on," he says.

He wanders off for a second, and comes back holding a rock the size of a grapefruit.

Right away, I know what he's doing: the Ol' Make Him Look. That's what Dan and I call any effort to take advantage of my dog's less-than-stellar intellect. Sometimes this is accomplished using a handful of nickels and dimes. Other times it's by giving a can of seltzer a good shake and then popping the top. And sometimes all you need is a nice enough rock.

"Kitty!" Dan shouts, waving the rock around. "Look, Kitty! Look what I've got!"

It's a nice enough rock to tear Kitty's attention away from Things & Stuff and the big, nasty Dumpster that he knows is right behind it. And a nice enough rock for us to lure the dog down the street and then on to a few more of the spots on our list of places where the missing robot might be.

11.

UNFORTUNATELY, THE SECOND HALF OF THE
afternoon goes just as poorly as the first.

Cheese Louise's is robot-less.

So is Country Joe's Fish.

And while Animal Chin's All-You-Can-Eat has seen plenty of ravenous customers over the past few days, it seems all of them have been of the human variety.

After that we make our way back to my house. We take a seat on the curb out front, and Dan gives Kitty the rock he's been waiting for all this time. The pooch squeals in excitement, traps the rock beneath a fuzzy paw, and then starts licking the thing like another dog might if it was made of pepperoni.

And then we just sit there—Dan, Edsley, and me.

We're silent.

Well, Dan and I are.

Edsley's making plenty of noise.

He got himself some mozzarella sticks at Cheese

Louise's, and then a fish sandwich at Country Joe's, and now he's inhaling them like he's competing in a speed-eating contest against himself.

Kitty, meanwhile, is still busy slobbering all over his rock.

Between him and Edsley, it's like a symphony of disgustingness.

It's a gross but appropriate soundtrack for my gloomy, hopeless mood.

12.

DAN AND EDSLEY GO HOME.

But only an hour or so later, Dan calls me up.

"Ken," he says.

"Dan," I say.

"I've been thinking," he tells me.

"Always a good sign," I tell him. "*What* have you been thinking?"

"Maybe . . . ," he starts.

But then doesn't finish.

"Maybe what?" I press.

"Maybe the bot really *isn't* responsible for all this stuff that's been happening."

The way he leaves it hanging, I can tell he's got more to say.

And for a second, I'm worried he's going to say that maybe it's *aliens* who are actually responsible for all of it.

Fortunately, he doesn't.

Instead he says, "I mean, it's not like they're

programmed to mess with power lines or satellites or anything like that."

"Sure," I say. "But they weren't programmed to fart speeding food-cubes, either. They weren't programmed to stomp on people's feet. Or sucker punch them in the gut. Or headbutt them. Or claw at their faces. Or—"

"Okay, okay," Dan says. "Point taken."

Silence.

Until Dan, sounding excited and hopeful, starts back up again.

"But—but it's been a couple of days now since anything else has happened. Say the blackout and the satellite and the Food-Plus *were* caused by the bot. He could've taken himself out of commission *after* all that."

"He could've," I admit. "But we'll never know for sure unless we find him. And finding him is the only way to make sure that down the road—next week, next month, next *year*—we don't get bitten in the backside. Remember?"

"I remember . . . ," says Dan, the excitement and hope already gone from his voice.

"Dan," I say, since I can see what he's getting at. "It'd be crazy to stop looking now. There're only a few more food places left on our list. The two of us can probably finish checking them out tomorrow afternoon."

"But what then?" Dan asks. "What if the bot's not at any of them, and *hasn't* been at any of them? Do we come up with *another* plan, and then spend the rest of the week doing *that*?"

"You said he couldn't have made it more than five miles from Edsley's. And I know there are a lot of other, non-food places within a five-mile radius of Edsley's. But not *so* many. I mean, it wouldn't take us *too* long to check them all out."

"But you just said it, Ken. The other bots did all sorts of things they weren't programmed to do. So yeah— Edsley's bot isn't programmed to go more than five miles away from his home base. But how can we be sure he hasn't?"

He gives me a second to turn the question over in my head before he answers it himself.

"We *can't*. For all we know, the bot's made it to another state. For all we know, he's in another *country*. Maybe he's roaming around Canada as we speak. And if that's the case, Ken . . . well, what are we supposed to do *then*?"

I gulp.

"If that's the case, Dan, then I think we better figure out how to contact the Canadian government."

13.

I HANG UP WITH DAN AND HEAD TO THE
kitchen. There, I stuff my face like *I'm* a bottomlessly hungry robot.

Maybe it's stress.

Or maybe I've just been spending too much time with Edsley.

All I know is that I'm starving.

So I gobble down a banana, then cram a granola bar in my mouth while I fix myself a bigger, better snack. My *favorite* snack: popcorn dipped in heated-up peanut butter. Not only is it delicious, but I'm hoping the warm, rich, salty-sweet awesomeness of the snack will cheer me up a bit.

I've got the preparation of it down to a science.

Or an art.

No, you know what?

A science *and* an art.

I grab a spoon and a jar of peanut butter and plop a hefty scoop of the stuff into a bowl. Then I get a bag of popcorn. I place them side by side in the microwave and set the thing to run for precisely one minute and fifty-six seconds.

Why?

Because I've done this dozens, probably even *hundreds* of times, and for the type of popcorn and the type of peanut butter my parents buy at the store, one minute and fifty-six seconds is *exactly* how long the popcorn needs to fully pop and the peanut butter needs to turn perfectly gooey.

Set the microwave for one minute and fifty-*five* seconds, and you'll be breaking your teeth on un-popped kernels and dipping the pieces that did pop into merely *semi*-gooey peanut butter.

Set it for one minute and fifty-*seven* seconds, and every few pieces of your popcorn will taste burnt and the peanut butter will scald your tongue.

I check to make sure I entered the time right.

And yep—the little screen on the microwave reads *1:56.*

So I press start.

And the microwave explodes.

14.

OKAY—SO THE MICROWAVE DOESN'T ACTUALLY *explode.*

But it *sounds* like it does, and even looks a little like it too.

First there's a *WHOOP!* that's loud enough to get Kitty abandoning his rock (which he insisted on bringing inside) and darting into the living room to take cover under the couch.

Then there's a pair of flashes, the first yellow-white and the second bright blue, like the color of fire at its hottest.

After that the microwave goes totally bonkers.

The light inside flashes off and on and off and on again, and the tray spins around so fast it looks like the bowl of peanut butter and bag of popcorn are on one of those vomit-tastic teacup rides they have at amusement parks.

And then there's the little screen. It's not counting

down from *1:56*. It's not doing *anything* that has to do with numbers.

ENNKNN

That's what it says.

Then:

GGOG

And then:

OTTOUTOU

It's at this point that I start to wonder whether a satellite is about to fall on my house.

15.

I RUSH OUTSIDE AND SCAN THE AREA FOR A

walking, talking, satellite-downing, microwave-exploding robot.

He's nowhere in sight, so I peer up into the sky.

Thankfully, nothing's plummeting out of it.

There's nothing up there at all.

Except for a cloud.

It's big. So big I can't even see all of it. The back half is blocked by my neighbor's roof.

Even in my panicked state, I can't help but think of John Henry Knox. Because this is just the sort of cloud the kid would go wild over. It might even be one of those cumulo-nimbo-whatchamacallits that showed up behind the Shop & Save on Saturday afternoon with all that rain and that he's been losing his mind over ever since. If the kid were here, he'd take a thousand pictures of the cloud. He'd chase it all around town, staring up at its bright white belly until he fried his retinas.

I consider calling him.

But then I remember that I'd been trying to cheer myself up, not drive myself nuts.

So I head back inside.

The microwave has stopped . . . doing whatever it was doing.

Still, I approach it cautiously, and open it nice and slow.

Then I put the bag of popcorn back in the cabinet— it didn't even begin to pop—and use the peanut butter to make myself a sandwich.

It's not as good as the snack I had in mind.

But at least I know a sandwich won't blow up on me.

16.

THAT NIGHT, I HAVE A BUNCH OF DREAMS.

Scratch that—I have a bunch of *nightmares*.

Every single one of them stars the missing robot.

In the first, the guy's right there in my bedroom with me, cramming everything he can into his stomach.

He goes for my lamp.

Then for a few of my books.

After that it's my wallet, and then my house keys, and then the prickly little cactus that my aunt gave me last year for my birthday and that, even though I haven't watered the thing once, refuses to die.

Finally, the bot swings his stomach-flap shut, crushes all my belongings into cubes, spins around, and pokes his butt in my direction.

I wake up just before he starts firing.

But not long after that, I find myself neck-deep in the next nightmare.

In this one, the robot's outside, charging around

town. He eats a skateboard, then a mailbox, and then a bike, growing larger with every additional snack. Within just a handful of seconds, he's big enough to eat cars. And then whole houses. And then the guy's swallowing up entire blocks.

That's it.

But this time, I don't even get a break before the next one.

Which features a whole group of giant robots. No, no, no—a whole *army* of them. They rampage around town, reducing everything to rubble with their turd-missiles of terror while satellites—*dozens* of them—rain down from the sky.

17.

MY NIGHTMARES FOLLOW ME TO SCHOOL

and cling to me all morning.

Worse, I start seeing the robot everywhere I look.

Not really, obviously.

Because that would actually be helpful.

But every time I turn a corner, I catch sight of the sun glinting off a mirror someone's got in their locker, or spot a kid's shiny silver backpack, and my brain goes into Panic Mode and I reach for my water bottle.

Oh yeah. Before I left the house this morning, I stuck a water bottle—a big one, filled to the brim—in my bag. Just in case.

By the time lunch rolls around, I'm feeling even worse than the guys all looked the day before.

I'm dejected.

Exhausted.

Beyond frazzled.

And honestly, a part of me wants to head to the

nurse's office instead of the room where the EngiNerds usually meet for lunch. Because I know if I tell him I'm feeling sick, he'll let me lie down on one of the cots he keeps in the back room. I figure I can snag another forty-five minutes of sleep, or at least just curl up into a ball and avoid things for a bit.

But before I can decide to run and hide from my problems, I have this sort of epiphany.

I say "sort of" because what occurs to me—it's not really earth-shattering. It's nothing I didn't already know when I woke up this morning. It's just that I'm all of a sudden seeing it in a new light, and it's this:

We're the EngiNerds.

And yes—I know I'm not the biggest fan of the name (or the silly motto). It would even be fair to say that I strongly dislike the name (and also the silly motto).

But still.

My friends, the guys *behind* the name?

They're brilliant.

A few of them might even be full-on geniuses.

And we've never, not ever, faced a problem that we couldn't solve. Because when we're not trying to one-up each other, when we're working together, all of us on the same team, there isn't a single thing we can't accomplish. I mean, we once launched a soda bottle six hundred feet up into the air using nothing but a baked potato and a can of hairspray. And a few of us once saved our town and possibly our state and arguably even a large chunk of our *country* from a horde of endlessly hungry, dangerously flatulent robots.

So I *don't* go down to the nurse's office.

I head to the room where I know the rest of the EngiNerds will be.

On my way there, I get all my thoughts in order. I outline a speech so good that as soon as the guys hear it, they're going to want to skip their afternoon classes and go robot-hunting with me right there and then.

"Gentlemen," I say as I step into the room, my hands up over my head to get everyone's attention. "I—"

But that's as far as I get.

Because that's when I see her.

Mikaela.

She's standing at the front of the room with a grin on her lips and a roller suitcase at her side.

"Gentlemen and *lady*," she corrects me.

18.

FOR A MINUTE, ALL I CAN DO IS STAND THERE
in the doorway and glare at Mikaela.

Because what is she *doing* here?

I thought I'd made it pretty clear that the EngiNerds weren't interested in any of her "extraterrestrial activity" nonsense.

But obviously, the girl's a little dense.

I guess I'll just have to make things even *clearer* for her.

So I stomp right up to her.

I get in her face.

"You come straight from the airport?" I say, jerking my chin at her suitcase.

She doesn't look at me, despite the fact that my face is about six inches from hers.

She doesn't answer my question, either.

What she does is say, "Don't do this."

"Do *what?*"

"Attempt to engage me in a battle of wits."

"Why's that?" I ask. "You don't think I have any *wit?*"

"No," she says, finally looking me in the eye. "In fact, I sincerely hope you do. It'd be nice if you had *something* of value, since you're clearly so deficient in the brain department."

My blood starts boiling. Seriously. I can hear the bubbles bobbing around and bursting in my veins.

"Look," I tell Mikaela, "I'll break this down for you, nice and simple. There aren't any aliens. Not in our town. Not *anywhere*. Which is why none of us"—I swing an arm out toward the rest of the guys—"want to sit around talking about them like there are. So, I'm gonna give you a chance, right now, before you humiliate yourself in front of all *my* friends, to get yourself and your silly little suitcase out of here."

Mikaela's grinning again.

Which, let me tell you, is absolutely maddening.

But then she loses the grin and puts on an exaggerated pout, pretending like my words have really hurt her—and this, believe it or not, is somehow even *more* infuriating.

"You mean you don't even want to see what's inside my silly little suitcase first?" she says.

"Not even a little bit," I tell her, doing my best to stay strong.

"Anyone else?" she calls out over my head.

It's loud enough for the handful of EngiNerds who haven't already noticed us to look over. The rest of them have been watching me and Mikaela ever since I stepped into the room.

"No?" she asks again, taking a step to the side so she can see the guys' faces. "I've got this big ol' suitcase, and there could be *anything* inside of it—anything at all. And you're saying I should just leave? Without even opening it up first? Without even giving you a peek?"

A few of the guys shrug.

Some of the others do some mumbling.

And that's good enough for Mikaela.

Before I can stop her, she's laying her suitcase down flat on the floor and unzipping the zippers. She pulls it open a second later, and sitting inside is literally the one thing

that us EngiNerds can't resist—it's kryptonite for our kind of nerdiness.

Gadgets.

That's what Mikaela has in her suitcase.

Lots and lots of gadgets.

My heart sinks.

We're done for.

19.

JOHN HENRY KNOX IS THE FIRST TO MAKE

his way over to Mikaela's suitcase. Staring down into it, he says, "May I?"

It's probably the politest thing that's ever come out of the kid's mouth, and hearing it gives me the shivers.

Mikaela holds a hand out to the gadgets heaped in her suitcase. "Dig in."

John Henry Knox doesn't hesitate. He moves aside something that looks like a stethoscope crossed with a hamster wheel, then something that looks like a meat thermometer with a spool of copper wire attached to it. After which he pulls out a large, incredibly complicated-looking object. It looks like a bunch of telescopes that have

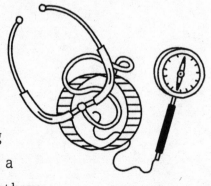

somehow been knotted together, and then decorated with more dials and levers and buttons and meters and knobs than any gadget—even *this* one—could possibly need.

"Is this what I think it is?" asks John Henry Knox.

"If you think it's a Gibson-Head 46X Multi-Scope," Mikaela says, "then *yes*."

John Henry Knox gasps. And the way he's gazing at the gadget, I'm expecting drool to start dribbling down his chin any second.

"I didn't even know they *made* a 46X . . . ," he says in a voice hushed with awe.

While John Henry Knox is busy falling in love with the multi-scope thingy, Mikaela gathers a bunch of other gadgets up in her arms and goes around the room passing them out to the guys. And as soon as they get those sleek, shiny pieces of metal into their hands, as soon as they have some dials to spin and some buttons to press, their faces light up.

Mikaela has just earned herself a permanent place in the guys' good graces.

She comes back to me last, still standing up front by her suitcase. And she's got one more gadget with her. It's a long, thin cylinder with a round, scooped dish on one side, sort of like an extra-large lollipop that's been dipped in lead.

Mikaela holds the thing out like she wants me to take it.

"What's *that* supposed to be?" I ask her.

She twists the gadget's handle in her fingertips so the dish part spins around and around, turning into a silvery blur.

"It's a data-eater," she says. "When you turn it on, it scans for zones of denser-than-normal data output. If it finds something, it vibrates." She lifts it up. "Like if you were standing next to a supercomputer—this bad boy would buzz like a hive of bees on sugar highs."

"A *data-eater*."

I say it like it's ridiculous, even though it sounds kind of awesome, and I can't help but think of all the things I could do with it.

"Name one time that's ever come in handy."

"Why stop at one?" Mikaela says. "I can give you five. I can give you *twenty*-five."

I give her a glare, then turn to face the rest of the room.

"Okay," I say, loud enough to penetrate the distracted

fog that the gadgets have thrust the guys into. "Thanks for stopping by, Mikaela, but show-and-tell time's over. We've got some more important matters to attend to."

The guys look from me to Mikaela, and then back at their gadgets.

"Let's go," I say, clapping a couple of times to get them moving.

But nobody does.

"Guys," I try again. "Come on."

And now none of them will even *look* at me.

John Henry Knox is marveling at the multi-scope.

Jerry's watching his reflection slip and slide over a small, polished sphere.

Amir's got a headset over his eyes.

Max and Alan are kneeling on the floor in front of a bunch of tubes and valves and sockets and sleeves.

Even Dan—he's completely captivated by a sleek silver tablet and its brightly glowing screen.

Mikaela shoves the data-eater into my hand while I'm not paying attention, then zips up her now-empty suitcase and rolls it out into the middle of the room.

"You guys can hang onto these for a bit," she says about the gadgets. "And if you want to talk about what's been going on around here lately, if you want to help me figure out how all the strange stuff that's been hap-pening is connected—if you want to be among the first Earthlings to ever make contact with extraterrestrial life . . ." She grins. "Well, just come and find me."

With that, she turns around and leaves.

"We won't!" I call after her.

She doesn't seem to hear me.

But it doesn't really matter.

I'm not even sure what I said is true.

20.

GETTING THE GUYS TO SET ASIDE THEIR

shiny new gadgets and pay attention to me for so much as half a second proves to be an impossible task.

Not even Dan will listen to me.

He pretends to—but I can tell he's actually focused on the flickering screen of the tablet he's still clutching.

Finally, I give up.

There are still fifteen minutes left in the lunch period, but I don't stick around for them.

I just leave.

And then, at the end of the day, I really *don't* stop by my locker.

There's no point.

I know none of the guys will be there waiting for me, ready to spend their afternoon slogging around town in search of the missing robot. And even if they *were*, I wouldn't want to see them. I'm serious. Let them have their fancy gadgets. Let them hang out with kooky girls and talk about *aliens*. I'll be better off on my own.

So when the last bell of the day rings, I leave class, head down the hall, and walk right out of the school's front doors.

But I don't make it much farther than that.

"KEN! WAIT UP!"

21.

OKAY, OKAY.

So maybe I lied a little bit back there.

Maybe it bummed me out more than I let on that none of the guys were willing to help me out anymore.

Maybe I really *did* wish they were all crowded around my locker, waiting for me to lay out a game plan and lead them into the afternoon.

And so, in the fraction of a second it takes me to turn around and see who rushed out of school behind me, shouting my name, my hopes soar. I decide it's Dan, and that he's here to apologize, and to tell me that he knows I'm mostly obsessing over this missing bot because I don't want it to come back to bite *him* in his backside and—

It's Edsley.

My hopes crash, burst into flame, and then explode in a giant fireball.

And then a sinkhole spontaneously forms on the

exact spot where my hopes crashed, and the poor things plunge even lower, all the way down to the molten-hot center of the earth, where they're instantly incinerated into nothingness.

"I was waiting for you," Edsley pants once he catches up to me, "at your locker. We going to find this bot, or what?"

I shake my head.

"No, Mike," I say, feeling even worse than I did two minutes ago. "I'm done. If no one else cares, then why should I? Why should I be driving myself nuts over this bot if no one else will even lift a finger to help me? Not even *Dan*."

Edsley frowns at me.

He looks genuinely confused.

"Ken . . . ," he says. "You're not *giving up*, are you?"

I clench my jaw and turn my head. I can't look him in the eye.

"We're *EngiNerds*, Ken," Edsley says. "We don't give up. We don't back down. When the going gets tough, we just get *tougher*. Maybe some of the other guys have forgotten that. But you and me—let's remind them. Let's show them how it's done."

Edsley's right, of course.

His pep talk is pretty much the same as the one I'd been planning on giving the guys at lunch.

And though I'm the only one there to hear it . . . it works.

It lifts my spirits.

Not as high as they *could* be.

But high enough for me to be persuaded.

"Okay," I tell Edsley. "Let's do this."

"*Let's*," he says, grinning and nodding his head. "And then," he adds, "when we're done, let's go celebrate with a pizza and some fries that maybe you'll pay for as a way of thanking me for my continued efforts."

I turn around and start off again.

"Fine," Edsley says, hurrying after me. "*I'll* buy the fries if you get the pizza. Ken? Ken! Do we have a deal?"

22.

"OW!" I SHOUT.

It's Kitty, doing his darnedest to yank my arm off again.

I wanted to leave him at home, seeing as he made it so difficult to get anything done the day before. But my mom had a friend over, and her friend was getting grossed out listening to Kitty mop up the kitchen floor with his tongue. Yes—the kitchen floor. Because in addition to rocks and dirty socks, the dog's got a thing for linoleum.

Speaking of dirty socks—Kitty's right back at it, same as yesterday. Edsley and I avoid Things & Stuff as best we can, but labradoodles must have some sort of big, nasty Dumpster detection system built into their brains, because as soon as we get within half a mile of the place, Kitty starts tugging me toward it.

And tugging me *hard*.

"Kitty!" I say, trying to sound as authoritative as I can

while I struggle to hang on to his leash. "Kitty, *stop*."

It doesn't work.

If anything, it makes Kitty tug me toward Things & Stuff even *harder*.

Then all of a sudden Edsley gasps.

"Oh man!" he cries, rushing a few feet past the dog and jabbing a finger toward the other end of the street. "Right there!"

I think he's doing what Dan did yesterday: the Ol' Make Him Look.

And it's working.

Kitty's whipping his head around, curious to see what Edsley's so excited about.

"Do it again," I say.

"No," Edsley says. "Ken. I'm serious. *Look*."

I look down the street in the direction he's pointing.

I don't see anything out of the ordinary.

Definitely no walking, talking, butt-blasting bot.

But Edsley must've seen the thing.

Because the next thing I know, he's charging down the street.

"HURRY, KEN!" he calls back to me. "IT'S GONNA GET AWAY!"

23.

EDSLEY BOLTS DOWN THE STREET.

I hurry after him. . . .

But only make it six feet.

Which is the length of Kitty's leash.

The pooch isn't budging.

Apparently he doesn't believe there's anything worth his while in the direction Edsley ran off.

The dog still wants to go to Things & Stuff.

"Kitty!" I shriek. "Come on! The robot! Edsley finally found the robot!"

Kitty throws his head back and gives a single, firm bark.

It's the canine equivalent of a toddler stomping their foot, which usually happens right before they throw a full-on tantrum.

I look for Edsley.

He's already made it around the corner and out of sight.

But faintly, in the distance, I can hear him.

"GRAB IT!" he's shouting. "IT'S MINE!"

"Kitty!" I cry, yanking at his leash again, and this time really leaning into it.

The dog plants his paws and growls.

"All right," I say. "You wanna do it the hard way?"

I rush at Kitty and, before he can slip away, scoop him up into my arms.

He squirms, trying to free himself.

But I hold him tight and hurry to catch up with Edsley.

No way am I letting Kitty get in the way of me finally finding this bot.

24.

I DON'T KNOW IF YOU'VE EVER TRIED TO GO
for a run while carrying an angry labradoodle, but let me tell you—it's not easy.

Kitty weighs ninety-three pounds.

He'd slow me down considerably even if he wasn't pawing me in the face, yapping in my ear, and doing everything else he can do to get me to stop taking him farther and farther away from Things & Stuff and his beloved big, nasty Dumpster.

By the time I get to the first corner that Edsley disappeared around, the kid has already disappeared around the *next*.

I pause and listen.

I can't hear Edsley, but I *do* hear a car horn honking.

And then someone else—an adult—shouting.

I head toward the commotion, first up one street and then down another, Kitty fighting me every step of the way.

25.

"MIKE!" I CALL OUT, AT LAST SPOTTING EDSLEY
in the distance.

He spins around and starts running toward me.

He doesn't have his missing robot with him.

But that's fine, I tell myself.

Because maybe he already doused the guy in water.

Maybe I couldn't hear the *SQUAH-POOM!* because
it happened while Kitty was yapping in my ear.

When Edsley gets a bit closer, I see that he's waving
something over his head.

A little piece of paper, it looks like.

It's green.

And crinkled.

"Check it out," he says once he reaches me. "I
thought it was a fifty. A five's still pretty sweet, though."

He means a five-dollar bill.

That's what he's holding.

"I had to run into traffic to get it," he tells me, "and

this old dude got *super* mad. But whatever. Free money!"

I look down at the five-dollar bill.

Then up at Edsley.

"Mike . . . ," I say—very, very slowly. "Is this what you were chasing after the whole time?"

He looks confused.

"Yeah, man," he says. "What did you think I—"

His mouth drops open into a big *O*.

"Oh dude. Did you think I found the robot?"

I set Kitty down on the sidewalk and pull him toward home.

"Ken!" Edsley calls out. "Where are you going, man?"

"Bye, Mike," I call back.

"Don't leave!"

I lift a hand.

Give him a wave.

"We can put the cash toward the pizza!" he says.

I don't answer.

Edsley keeps calling after me.

But eventually, I make it out of earshot.

26.

ON THE WAY HOME, I GUESS BECAUSE I DON'T
feel bad enough already, I dig Mikaela's data-eater out
of my backpack.

Kitty sees it, comes closer for a sniff—and immediately loses interest.

That's more or less how I feel about it too.

I probably should've flushed the thing down the toilet right after lunch, or at least tossed it in the trash.

I look around the street for a garbage can, thinking
I'll do just that, but don't find one before I make it home.

Stepping into the house, I unclip Kitty from his leash
and hear:

"What's *that?*"

I look up and see Mom standing there at the
kitchen counter. She's got a stack of mail in front of
her, but her eyes are fixed on the data-eater I've still
got in my hand.

"Oh, ah—"

I shove the gadget into my pocket.

"Nothing," I say.

Mom lifts an eyebrow, and for a second, I'm pretty sure she's going to do some prying.

But she fights off the urge, goes back to the mail, and then just tells me to make sure I get all my homework done before six o'clock, since that's when we have to leave.

"Leave?"

"For dinner," she tells me.

"What dinner?"

Mom drops the catalog she's holding. She narrows her eyes at me, like she's trying to figure out if I'm messing with her.

"The dinner," she finally says, "that I told you about a hundred times. At the Lins'. With the Knoxes."

I must make a face.

"What is it?" Mom says.

But what am I supposed to tell her?

That there's a farting robot on the loose and no one but me seems to care about finding it?

Or that some kooky, alien-obsessed girl is trying to steal all my friends?

Or that those friends—Jerry and John Henry Knox

included—seem totally cool with being stolen away
by her?

No, no, and *no*.

So I just say, "Nothing."

Again.

I don't stick around to see if Mom buys it.

I just hurry off to my room.

27.

I DON'T ACTUALLY GET ANY HOMEWORK

done that afternoon.

No, I spend the hour or so I've got before my parents and I have to leave for Jerry's trying to figure out how I can get out of going.

I could say I'm sick. . . .

But that might have some unwanted repercussions, like being made to gargle salt water or go to bed super early.

It's almost June, so I could say I've got a big end-of-the-year project I need to start working on. . . .

But then my mom and dad would ask a bunch of questions about the project, and check in on my progress, and want to see the final product, and I'm not sure it's worth doing all of that extra, unnecessary work just to get out of spending a couple of hours with Jerry and John Henry Knox.

And that's when I start to convince myself that maybe it won't be so bad.

Sure, things have been a bit strained among us lately.

And lunch that day was, in a word, terrible.

But for all I know, the guys had their fun with Mikaela's fancy gadgets and then gave them back to her at the end of the day. And maybe they then took that opportunity to explain to Mikaela what I'd been trying to tell her all along—that the EngiNerds' nerdiness doesn't extend outside the realm of reality, that we don't believe in *aliens*. Maybe a night of hanging out—just me, Jerry, and John Henry Knox—is what we need to set things straight and get us all back on the right track.

So when six o'clock rolls around, I get in the car and head to the Lins' house with my parents, actually feeling sort of hopeful about the evening I've got ahead of me. And when we arrive, I do what I normally do whenever I go to Jerry's: I kick off my shoes, say hi to his mom and dad and little brother, and then head right up to his bedroom.

But there, things stop being normal.

I don't go in, grab a magazine or a game controller, and plop down on one of Jerry's beanbags.

I stop short in the doorway.

Because Jerry and John Henry Knox are at Jerry's

desk—and on top of it are a whole bunch of Ms. The-Truth-Is-Out-There's gadgets.

One of them is the multi-scope that John Henry Knox got all gaga over at lunch.

Jerry, meanwhile, is fiddling with something that looks like a flashlight. But not just any old ordinary flashlight. The thing's got all these extra knobs and buttons along the shaft. It looks like the sort of contraption a superhero might carry around—a flashlight that doubles as a grappling hook or folds out into a scooter.

It's Jerry who finally notices me standing in the doorway.

"Oh, um . . . hey," he says.

John Henry Knox is too focused on the multi-scope to even look up.

Jerry spends a minute ping-ponging his eyes back and forth from me to the gadgets. Then he rolls open one of his desk drawers and, reaching inside, pulls out a pair of small, brown, familiar-looking cartons.

"Chocolate milk?" he says, holding a carton out to me.

It's a peace offering.

Jerry's way of acknowledging the awkwardness between us, but also asking a fairly profound question:

If we can't sit down and enjoy a carton of chocolate milk together, then what has the world come to?

28.

I HEAD INTO JERRY'S ROOM AND TAKE A

seat.

I also take the carton of chocolate milk he offered me.

I stab the straw through the foil top and suck up a sip, careful not to look like I'm enjoying the beverage *too* much. I don't want the guys to read it as me approving of whatever they're doing with Mikaela's gadgets.

Frustratingly, though, I can't figure out just what that *is*.

It's clear they're working toward something, that they've got a goal.

But all I can tell is that it seems to involve fastening Jerry's flashlight to John Henry Knox's multiscope.

They're using dental floss to do the fastening. I can smell the minty scent coming off the thin, slightly sticky thread.

Working together, they finally get the flashlight fixed in place.

And then Jerry's on his feet, racing over to his window and sliding it up.

John Henry Knox is right on his heels, carrying the fastened-together gadgets with a mix of apprehension and excitement.

Jerry helps position the gadgets on the windowsill, after which John Henry Knox begins to crank the knobs and spin the dials of the multi-scope. He pauses now and again to let Jerry press a button on his flashlight, and then gets right back to cranking and spinning.

This goes on long enough for me to see that each button on Jerry's flashlight corresponds to a different color. Press *this* one, and the gadget sends a shaft of orange light shooting up into the sky. Press *that* one, and out comes a bright beam of purple.

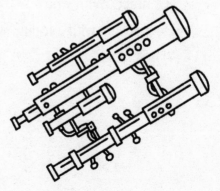

Orange.

Purple.

Blue.

Green.

Purple again.

Back to orange.

Then Jerry and John Henry Knox wait.

They just sit there for a minute, peering up into the cloudless sky.

After which they do it all over again.

Orange, purple, blue, green, purple, orange.

I watch them do the whole thing five times in a row, still trying to figure out what they're up to.

But I can't.

So finally, I ask.

It's John Henry Knox who says, "We're attempting to make contact."

I still don't get it.

"Contact? With who?"

He answers with a totally straight face:

"The aliens."

29.

MAKE *CONTACT?*

With *aliens?*

Are they *joking?*

I look around, half expecting some of the other EngiNerds to pop out of Jerry's closet and tell me this is all some gag.

But instead, lying there on Jerry's desk among the rest of Mikaela's gadgets, I see a piece of paper with *From the Desk of M. Harrington* printed at the top. Beneath the header are some sketches and instructions. I recognize the multi-scope. And the flashlight. And then I find the color sequence, *orange—purple—blue—green—purple—orange*, written out in what must be Mikaela's handwriting, after which she added, *pause—repeat as necessary.*

"Guys," I say, turning back to Jerry and John Henry Knox, "come on. I know this girl's got some cool toys and all"—I flick my fingers at the gadgets—"but please tell me she doesn't have you actually believing all this stuff about *aliens*."

Jerry shrugs.

"Honestly? I'm not sure *what* I think anymore."

John Henry Knox clears his throat.

"Here's what *I* think," he says, and because the kid is incapable of giving a simple, straightforward answer, he launches into a full-on lecture. "The universe is extraordinarily vast, and every second it's growing even vaster. Our knowledge of it is extremely limited. Say, for instance, that Jerry's bedroom here is the universe."

Jerry looks around his bedroom, and after a second, so do I.

John Henry Knox, meanwhile, leans over and plucks a single fiber out of the carpet. Sitting back up, he lifts the bit of string into the light, but it's so tiny, I can still barely see it.

"In the Jerry's-bedroom-as-the-universe analogy," John Henry Knox goes on, "this nearly nonexistent strand of thread would be our galaxy, the Milky Way. And our solar system? Our center-of-everything sun, our planet and its neighbors, the asteroid belt and all the comets flying about? It would be but a single atom of dust clinging to this nearly nonexistent strand of thread."

John Henry Knox looks at me meaningfully.

"Do you have a point?" I ask him. "Or are you just trying to destroy Jerry's carpet?"

He flicks the thread to the floor.

"My *point* is that there's so, so, *so* very much we don't know. So, so, *so* very much we haven't seen." He gestures around Jerry's room. "To make a definitive statement about something you have absolutely zero knowledge of—well, it's foolish. It's *beyond* foolish. It's downright absurd!"

It takes me a second to gather my thoughts.

My head feels all fuzzy.

It's hard to fit infinity into your brain.

It's hard, and even a little bit scary, to conceive of the whole wide world as being just a part of a speck of dust on a single, itty-bitty piece of string.

"Okay," I finally say. "Okay, *fine*. But that doesn't mean you have to waste your time trying to *make contact*. There are better things you could be doing. Like, oh, I don't know—helping your friend find the last of the farting robots that's still on the loose and is causing all sorts of craziness in your town so that said farting robot doesn't figuratively and/or *literally* bite us all in the backside."

"I suppose it's a matter of opinion just what consti-tutes a *waste of time*," says John Henry Knox.

I eye him.

"What's that supposed to mean?"

He looks at me like I'm an idiot. Which isn't unusual, but is particularly annoying at the moment.

"The definition of insanity—" he begins.

"I know, I know," I tell him. "But that doesn't change the fact that this bot's still out there, still—"

"We're ninety-eight percent certain that none of the 'craziness' you mentioned was caused by Edsley's missing robot," John Henry Knox interrupts. And once he's sure I'm not going to re-interrupt *him*, he adds, "We're also ninety-*nine* percent certain that the bot, even if he's still operational, no longer poses a threat to the community."

"Who's *we*?" I ask.

"All of us," says John Henry Knox. "Me, Jerry, Dan, Max, Amir, Simon, Alan, Chris, Rob. And Mikaela, of course. She showed us what she's been working on after school today. She's linked all the strange happenings in town—the blackout, the satellite, the Food-Plus—to a series of strikingly similar weather patterns. We ended up telling her about the bot, and she helped us run some scenarios and crunch some numbers. Which is how we came to be nearly certain that there's no reason to be *wasting our time* looking for it. Which is why we're now working on *this*."

With that, John Henry Knox returns his attention to the gadgets on the windowsill. It's like he's decided that talking to me any further is a waste of time too.

I sit there for a moment, shell-shocked, then get to my feet and make a beeline for the door.

"Ken—" Jerry says.

But there's nothing more I need to hear.

I storm down the hall and into the bathroom, where I pace back and forth from the toilet to the sink, my blood pumping harder with every trip.

I can't believe my friends have all gone from level-headed to loony in the space of a single afternoon.

And I can't believe *Mikaela*.

She wheeled her stupid little roller suitcase into my life like the Trojan Horse, unpacking all her fancy gadgets and then tearing my world apart.

30.

I FAKE SICK.

It's lame, I know.

But I don't know what else to do.

All I know is that I can't spend the rest of the night hanging out with Jerry and John Henry Knox, trying to *make contact*.

So after fuming in the bathroom for a bit, I head downstairs.

I slump my shoulders, sag my lips, and do everything else I can to make myself look as pitiful as possible.

It works.

I don't even have to say a thing.

I just shuffle into the living room, which is where my mom and dad are hanging out with Jerry's and John Henry Knox's parents. As soon as Mrs. Lin sees me she says, "Ken? Is everything okay?"

My dad's on his feet a beat later.

"You look sick," he says. "Do you feel sick?"

He presses the back of his hand to my forehead, then turns to my mom.

"He feels warm."

I'm not surprised.

But I know it's not an actual fever that's got me all heated up.

It's a feverish *rage*.

Mom and Dad don't need to know that, though.

So I keep my mouth shut, and stand aside while they apologize to Jerry's and John Henry Knox's parents about having to miss dinner and take me home.

I make sure to move sluggishly, first through the house and then out to the car. I climb into the backseat and set my forehead against the window, hoping the cool glass might slow down my thoughts, which are crashing and bashing around in my head like a bunch of little kids in bumper cars.

My mom drives fast, probably because she's afraid I'm going to vomit.

The trees whiz by, turning into dark, frilly blurs.

The sky, clear and dark, is alive with stars.

The sight makes all of what John Henry Knox said

come back to me. The stuff about the vastness of the universe, and our extremely limited knowledge of it, and how—

That's when I see it, looming up above.

A cloud.

One that looks just like the cloud I saw in my backyard the day before, right after my microwave spectacularly malfunctioned, and just like the cloud that came to the rescue last weekend behind the Shop & Save, dumping down rain right in the nick of time and making the last of the robots we were facing off against go *SQUAH-POOM!* It's one of those cumulo-nimbo-majigs—a big white behemoth the size of a shopping mall and shaped like a gigantic, cotton ball–covered anvil.

Or like a *UFO*.

I tilt my head to try to get a better view of the thing.

I peer up at its wide white belly, so bright it seems to glow with its very own light.

And then, as I'm staring up at it, the bright whiteness begins to change.

It starts to look . . .

Well, *orange*.

I blink.

But the orange is still there. It's like looking at a

gargantuan clementine through a thick layer of fog.

I shut my eyes and squeeze them tight.

And when I open them back up, the orange is finally gone.

But the cloud hasn't gone back to being white.

Now it's looks *purple*.

The next thing I know, I'm pounding on my parents' headrests.

"PULL OVER!" I shout. "PULL OVER!"

31.

I HOP OUT OF THE CAR AS SOON AS IT STOPS.

"Not on your shoes, Ken!" my mom calls after me. "No puking on your new shoes!"

I run a short ways down the road, to a spot where I can better see the cloud through the trees.

It's drifting away, off in the direction of Jerry's house, its belly no longer right above me. And seeing it like this, from an angle, the portion of the cloud that a second ago looked purple now looks more gray—a color it's completely normal for a cloud to be.

My breathing slows.

My thoughts settle.

And then I understand that the cloud never was orange, and that I didn't then watch it turn purple.

Obviously.

I've just been exposed to too much of Mikaela's kookiness.

And just like all the rest of the EngiNerds, it's got me

thinking impossible things, and even *seeing* impossible things.

Feeling like Kitty must feel after falling for the Ol' Make Him Look, I trudge back to the car and get in.

Mom cranes her neck to get a look at my feet.

"You going to be okay?" she asks me, satisfied I haven't ruined my shoes.

I tell her the truth:

"I'm not sure."

32.

AT HOME, I CALL UP DAN.

"Dan," I say, like always.

But he must hear it in my voice—the confusion, the hurt.

"Ken. Uh, hey. How's it, um . . . going?"

"Wonderful," I lie.

Because this isn't about me.

This is about him.

And all the rest of the guys.

And *Mikaela*.

"How's it going with *you*?" I ask. And then, quickly deciding that this leaves him too much wiggle room, I get right to the point: "What'd you do after school today?"

I can hear him swallow.

He knows I know. And I know he knows I know.

I also know that he's on the other end of the line gnawing on his lip, and that, if I let him, he'll go on gnawing for the next ten minutes while he tries to figure out what to say.

Well, he can gnaw that lip right off his face for all I care.

I've got enough to say for the both of us.

"Dan," I begin, "don't you see that this is just like last time? John Henry Knox started sharing his kooky conspiracy theories about the weather, about apocalyptic megastorms and the meaning of *clouds*, and you gobbled it all up. You went home and built yourself a fleet of farting robots. And now you're buying into all this alien stuff. Now you're spending your time trying to *make contact*. So what's next, Dan? Huh? What giant mess are you gonna make *this* time?"

"Ken," Dan says, "I know you and John Henry Knox have your differences, but if you don't think something weird's been going on with the weather . . ."

"Then *what*?"

"Well, then *you* might be the kooky one."

I open my mouth to defend myself, but Dan starts up again before I can.

"Just *think* about it," he says. "Remember the hail storm last week? And then all that rain behind the Shop & Save? I know you might not want to believe it, I know you'll probably never admit it—but John Henry Knox was right. He *is* right. Something's definitely going on. I don't know if it's apocalyptic. I don't know if all this weird weather means the world is about to end. But—"

"But you think it might mean that there are aliens in our town," I interrupt. "Is that what you're saying? That if there really, truly are aliens out there in the universe, you think they'd use their super advanced technology to come to our little planet, to our little town, and cause a couple of storms?"

"I think—"

"And what about the *robot*, Dan? The one we know for a fact *is* really and truly out there, and that I've been driving myself nuts trying to find for the past week so that it doesn't fart someone to smithereens, get traced back to you, and get you in a ton of trouble?"

"He's *not* going to do anything," Dan says, and then he gives me the same line John Henry Knox did. "We're ninety-eight percent certain that Edsley's bot hasn't been responsible for any of what's been going on in town, and ninety-nine percent certain that he's not a threat."

And there it is again.

That "*we*."

Meaning the EngiNerds.

Plus Mikaela.

Minus me.

"Unless someone actively antagonizes him," Dan goes on, "the bot's going to keep doing whatever he's doing. Lying in a ditch. Roaming around Canada. Or—or, I don't know . . . working at a shoe store."

"Working at a *shoe store*?"

If I was in a better mood, I'd laugh at the idea of one of these butt-blasters being gainfully employed.

Dan takes a breath.

"Ken," he says, "you're one of the most stubborn people I know. And before you start stubbornly telling me that you're *not* stubborn," he's quick to add, "just please—*listen*."

He waits to make sure I'm going to.

"Sometimes, Ken, your stubbornness can be a good thing. A *great* thing, even. Like when you're facing a tough problem. You don't give up. But sometimes, in other situations . . . well, I wish you'd just give *in*. Maybe Mikaela's right about the aliens. Maybe she's wrong. All I know is that she's smart. *Really* smart. And the stuff she has to say, all the things she showed us—it's fascinating, man. It's *exciting*. And it makes a lot of sense. If you'd just let your guard down and give her a chance, I think you'd think so too. I *know* you would. And if it'd make you feel better, I'm sure she'd help us find Edsley's bot, wherever he is. I mean, the girl's got a gadget for everything."

I jump on this last thing, since it's the easiest, least uncomfortable part of what he said to respond to.

"Fancy gadgets," I tell him, "aren't always the answer."

"I know it," says Dan. "The human brain is the best gadget around. No contest. But now and again, it can use a little help."

I guess I agree with that.

But I'm not about to come out and say it.

So I keep my mouth shut.

And so does Dan.

And the silence builds, stretching on and on and leaving me to wonder what in the world has happened to us.

Last week, I found out that Dan's been lying to me for the past two years, all while secretly building a fleet of robots in his basement. And now, somehow, he's over all that. He's already moved on to the next thing— Mikaela and her aliens.

And maybe, I can't help but think, he's moving on from *me*.

This thought throws everything else into question.

Maybe, I suddenly find myself wondering, the bot really *isn't* responsible for the blackout and the satellite and the Food-Plus.

Maybe my worries have been misplaced.

Maybe I'm obsessing over this missing robot, and obsessing over Dan helping me look for him, because all along, deep down, I've known what's happening. I've noticed the two of us drifting apart, bit by bit growing more and more distant, until finally the gap between us is just too big to be bridged. Because in seemingly no time at all, we've gone from best friends to regular friends within a larger group to the sort of friends who keep secrets from each other to, well, whatever we are now. A couple of kids who don't see eye to eye. Who don't believe the same things. Who have totally different ideas about how they should be spending their time.

"Ken . . ."

I hang up.

It's a pathetic, cowardly move—even lamer than faking sick to get out of doing something you don't want to do.

But I don't know what else to do.

Sitting there staring at the phone, I feel lost.

The things I thought were true, and thought always would be true, suddenly aren't. It's like someone telling you that north is actually south, that right is in fact left, that the earth doesn't orbit the sun but is just out there, spinning fast and loose without anything to keep it from crashing into Venus or Mars.

I'm a smart kid. But right now, I feel like I don't know anything at all.

33.

THAT NIGHT, EDSLEY'S MISSING ROBOT IS once again waiting for me in my dreams.

This time, though, he's not gobbling up everything in sight and downing satellites.

He's just standing there on a street corner beside a big red STOP sign.

Dream Me takes a step toward him.

Then another.

Followed by one more.

There, the robot points.

Not at me.

But straight up at the sky.

I look, and see a giant cloud—a cumulonimbus, of course.

A spot toward the cloud's center begins to swirl, and a hollow space opens up. It's shaped like a mouth.

Because, I find out a moment later, it *is* a mouth.

"Kennedy," the cloud says.

And because I can't seem to have a pleasant dream to save my life, the cloud's voice is identical to John Henry Knox's.

"You must try to fit infinity into your brain . . . ," the cloud commands me.

And then again:

"You *must* try to fit infinity into your brain. . . ."

And again, even more insistently:

"You MUST try to fit infinity into your brain. . . ."

Until finally, the thing's just shouting down at me.

"DO IT ALREADY, KENNEDY. FIT INFINITY INTO THAT PUNY LITTLE BRAIN OF YOURS. HURRY UP AND GET. IT. DONE."

34.

I WAKE UP SEVERAL MINUTES BEFORE MY
alarm is set to squawk.

Normally, I'd turn over and get a little more sleep.

But there's no way I'm doing that—not with John
Henry the Cumulonimbus hanging out in my dreams.

So I get up, get dressed, and head to my desk to get
my school stuff. I'm reaching for my notebook when I
see it:

The data-eater.

The sight of the gadget fills me with all sorts of
uncomfortable, conflicting feelings. I don't know what
to do with the thing. For whatever reason, I don't really
feel like flushing it down the toilet or tossing it in the
trash anymore. But at the same time, I don't want it
sitting in my room.

I stick the gadget into my pocket, figuring I can think
about what to do with it on my way to school—right
after I think about where I'm going to eat lunch that

day, since I'm pretty sure it won't be in the room I regularly eat along with the rest of the EngiNerds. Then I sling my backpack over my shoulder and head for the door. But halfway there, something in the window catches my eye.

I turn and look—and look and look.

But all the looking in the world won't help me make sense of what I'm seeing.

Snow.

And a whole lot of it.

My lawn, the street, the roofs of all the neighbors' houses—all of them are covered in the stuff.

Overnight, the world has been made smooth, bright, and sparkling white.

It's almost summer.

But outside it's a winter wonderland.

35.

I DON'T KNOW HOW LONG I STAND THERE GAPING
out my window at all the snow. It must be a while, though,
because eventually my mom comes up to check on me.

"Freak blizzard," she says.

The words lodge themselves deep in my mind.

"That's what they're calling it on channel five," she
goes on. "Apparently it was dumping down all night."

I hear a familiar sound—a harsh, chunky scraping.
I realize what it is just before the plow truck comes
around the corner. I watch it carve a dark path down
the center of the otherwise blindingly white street.

"And guess what?" Mom says.

I can hear the smile in her voice.

"School's canceled," she says. "You have a snow day,
Ken—in May!"

Before I can even begin to wrap my head around all
of this, Mom says something else:

"Oh, and Mike's waiting for you downstairs."

36.

I FIND EDSLEY IN THE KITCHEN.

He's standing there in his boots and snow pants, a toasted waffle in one hand and a bottle of syrup in the other.

I watch him dump half the bottle of syrup onto the waffle, then try to cram the whole thing into his mouth.

It's messy.

And more than a little gross.

"Oooh aah," he says, chunks of chewed-up waffle tumbling out of his mouth and down onto the floor.

"What?"

Edsley mashes his mouthful a few more times, then forces it down his throat.

"Snow day," he says, hooking a syrup-covered thumb over his shoulder. "My sled's out front."

On snow days, the EngiNerds always do the same thing. We get our snow gear on, grab our sleds—all of which we've either built ourselves or elaborately remodeled, of course—and meet at the hill behind the high school.

But I can't do that.

I can't go about the day like everything's normal, like life's just fine and dandy.

I mean, the rest of the EngiNerds are out there trying to *contact aliens*, and we just had a freak blizzard of absolutely epic proportions in *May*. My mind is a mess. I don't think I've got the wherewithal to even eat breakfast before I set some things straight.

Before I can figure how to explain all this to Edsley, there's a *whoosh*, and a gust of cold air crashes over me.

My stomach sinks.

"Mike . . . ," I say. "What's the one thing I always tell you to do as soon as you step foot in my house?"

Edsley doesn't hesitate:

"Close the door behind me," he says. "Duh."

It takes him another second.

At which point he whips around and gapes at the door standing wide open behind him.

"Oh," he says. "My bad."

37.

THERE'S NO NEED TO SEARCH THE HOUSE

for Kitty.

The dog has a sixth sense when it comes to open front doors. If you leave one cracked so much as a hair's breadth, he'll know—and he won't waste any time wriggling himself out of it.

So I head straight for the door, my imagination already cooking up scenarios about where the pooch could be, each one more worst-case than the last.

Outside, the porch, front steps, and walkway are all still covered in snow, making it easy to see the trail of Kitty-size paw prints leading across the one, down the other, and then all the way out to the sidewalk.

I follow them for another half a block.

But there the trail goes cold.

Because *some* Good Samaritan decided to get out of bed at the crack of dawn, crank up their snow blower, and clear off not only *their* sidewalk, and not only their neighbor's sidewalk, but their neighbor's *neighbor's* sidewalk, and their neighbor's neighbor's *neighbor's* sidewalk too.

I turn around and hurry back toward home, figuring I'd better put together my usual kit of Kitty search-and-rescue items: a box of tissues, as much loose change as I can find, a can of seltzer, the dog's favorite dirty sock—

It's then that I finally realize where Kitty is.

Things & Stuff.

Or, to be precise, *behind* Things & Stuff.

There's no doubt in my mind that the pup is back there in that parking lot, whining and yapping and doing his darnedest to cram his big, fluffy—and, as of that morning, *clean*—body under that big, nasty Dumpster.

38.

I GET TO THINGS & STUFF AS FAST AS I CAN,
but thanks to all the snow soaking through my sneakers
and numbing my toes, not to mention all the invisible
patches of ice that keep threatening to sweep my legs
out from under me, it's seriously slow going.

It'd probably help if I could actually pay attention to
where I'm walking.

But I'm having some trouble doing that.

Surrounded by piles and heaps and even a couple
mini-mountains of snow, my mind keeps wandering.

I'm thinking about this mid-May snowstorm, this
freak blizzard, and how that's the same word John
Henry Knox has been using when discussing the out-
of-nowhere downpour that saved our butts from the
bots behind Shop & Save on Saturday afternoon. A
freak storm—that's what he's been calling it. And now it
seems there's been a second one.

I peer up into the cloud-covered sky—and slip on another patch of ice.

I steady myself just before I fall.

Focus, I tell myself.

I take a deep breath.

Clear my head.

And pay attention to where I'm walking the rest of the way to Things & Stuff.

When I finally get there, I hear Kitty before I even make it around to the back of the store.

He's yapping and whining and making a series of other noises that the untrained ear might assume were coming from a wounded sea lion instead of a totally healthy dog.

I go around back and find Kitty exactly where I knew he'd be. He's pawed the snow away from in front of the big, nasty Dumpster, and has been attempting to squeeze himself into the two-inch gap between it and the dirty pavement of the parking lot. He's been at it for no more than five minutes, but his belly, which is usually fluffy and golden brown, is already all matted and black. His head, meanwhile, looks like it was dunked in oil, plus there's a banana peel stuck to his back.

"Dude," I say to him.

Kitty gives me a yap, then once again tries to cram himself under the Dumpster.

I rush over and yank him back before he can get any messier, if such a thing is even possible. Then, choosing the least disgusting spot on the grimy ground in front of the Dumpster, I get down on my knees and peer beneath it.

Something's definitely there.

And whatever it is, I know Kitty's not going to let me take him home until he gets it.

So I stick my arm under the Dumpster and drag the thing out.

And what is it?

A sock.

A very, very dirty sock.

It's an exact match for the one Kitty has back home.

This is what he's been so desperate to get these past few days.

I toss the sock to the dog, and as soon as he's got the disgusting thing clamped between his teeth, he leaps into the air, spins in circles, rolls around in the snow, and just generally goes nuts.

I don't think I've ever seen the guy so happy.

39.

I LET KITTY HAVE A MOMENT WITH HIS SOCK.

Then I give his leash a tug and we start off.

My plan is to head home.

If Edsley is either dumb or bold enough to still be there, I'm going to drag him outside and not-so-gently dunk his head into the snow.

But I don't make it home.

I don't even make it more than a dozen steps.

Just as I get back around to the front of Things & Stuff, something strange happens.

My leg—it starts shaking like crazy.

It freaks me out a bit.

Okay, fine—it freaks me out a *lot*.

And maybe, just maybe, I let out a little shriek.

Because it's not until I set a hand on my wildly vibrating hip that I remember what's in my pocket.

The data-eater.

40.

I SPOT A STOP SIGN AT THE CORNER, JUST A handful of feet from Things & Stuff.

I pull Kitty over to it and tie his leash to the pole.

Then I dig the data-eater out of my pocket.

The thing's going crazy. The top part of it, the little dish—it's shaking so fast the edges are a blur, and if I hold on to the handle part too hard, the vibrations run through my wrist and down into the bones of my arm.

I hold the gadget out toward Things & Stuff, and it feels like the shaking intensifies. I pull it back, and it seems, just slightly, to weaken.

I try to remember what Mikaela told me about the data-eater. Something about it scanning for zones of "denser-than-normal data output." And the example she gave, about how if you stood next to a super-computer, the thing would "buzz like a hive of bees on sugar highs."

Turning the gadget over, I find a tiny switch. It's not

marked, but I flip it anyway, and the shaking begins to slow.

As soon as the data-eater stops buzzing, I stick it back into my pocket and head right up to Things & Stuff. The store's front is made up entirely of windows, but the place is so cluttered with racks of things and shelves of, well, *stuff* that it's nearly impossible to see inside.

I try to anyway, stepping up to the window and popping onto my toes to peer over a tower of magazines blocking my view. I see glitzy cell phone covers and cheap plastic sunglasses and hairbrushes that look like they've definitely had more than one previous owner, some of them possibly of the feline variety, but nothing else out of the ordinary.

I'm about to stop there—to turn around, grab Kitty, and continue home. But then I hear Dan in my head. All those things he said about Mikaela being brilliant and me being stubborn. About how she might even have a gadget that could help us finally find the missing bot.

I take a deep breath—and make a decision.

I'm going to listen to Dan.

I'm going to *give in*.

I'm going to believe, at least temporarily, that Mikaela's gadget has detected *something* interesting inside Things & Stuff, whether or not it's the walking, talking, butt-blasting bot that's been eluding me for nearly a week.

And so I push open the door and head into the store.

A little bell dings above me.

Half a second later, I hear it—the flat, cold, emotionless tones of a robot:

"WEL-come to THINGS and Stuff. How may I HA . . . HA . . . HELP *youuu?*"

 41.

IT'S HIM.

The missing robot.

I don't need Edsley there to confirm it.

He looks just like Greeeg, the bot Dan sent me last week—before I fed the guy a water balloon and *SQUAH-POOM*ed him into a heap of nuts and bolts and overripe bananas, that is.

The bot's down at the far end of the store, a stapler pinched in one claw and a salad spinner dangling from the other. He places the items on a shelf beside a 1,000-count package of those fuzzy little circles you stick on the bottoms of chair legs, then comes down the aisle toward me.

It's only then that I see the sticker on his shiny torso. HELLO, it says. MY NAME IS: KLAUS.

"GREE-tings cus-TOM-er," the bot says once he reaches me. "You are my FIRST cus-TOM-er."

Customer?

I have to read the bot's sticker another couple times before the ridiculous realization finally fixes itself in my brain. The bot, Klaus—he *works* here. And I guess it does make a certain sort of twisted sense. The bot's *were* programmed to help people.

As if proving this point, Klaus repeats what he said when I first stepped into the store:

"How may I HA . . . HA . . . HELP *youuu*?"

I consider the question. And of course the thing that I've been eager to do all week—serve the bot the same last meal I served Greeeg—comes right to mind. But I can't really tell Klaus that he can help me out by permanently ending his career as a Things & Stuff employee, can I? I can't tell him that I'd like nothing more than to shove him into a swimming pool and turn him into a bunch of harmless scrap metal and once-compressed comestibles.

Speaking of which—I'm totally unarmed.

I quickly scan the racks and shelves on either side of me, but I can't find any bottles of water. The only liquid-y thing I see, between a sombrero and an umbrella with a pickle-shaped handle, is a jug of laundry detergent. But would that even work? Would that make Klaus go *SQUAH-POOM*?

"Will you be MAK-ing a PUR-chase on this FINE *daaay*?"

The tinted round pieces of plastic that are the robot's eyes flicker rapidly.

He's excited.

Like he's been waiting days for his very first customer to walk into the store.

"Um," I say, looking over the racks and shelves again. Because if buying something from the bot will buy me a little more time to figure out what to do, I'm more than happy to make a purchase.

Finally, I spot a pocket thesaurus. It's cheap, and pretty much the only thing in the store I can ever imagine actually using.

I go to grab it as Klaus scoots behind the cash register.

"One POCK-et the-SAUR-us," he says as I make my way to the counter. "That WILL be two DOLL . . . DOLL . . ."

"Dollars?" I offer.

"Two DOLL-ars and FIF-tee *ceeents*," the bot finishes.

I reach for my wallet—and a door at the back of the store bangs open, smacking the wall behind it so hard I literally jump. A man storms out. It's Stan. And when the kid-hating owner of Things & Stuff sees me standing there in his store, he assumes the worst. I can tell just from the way he glares at me that he thinks I'm there to cause some major trouble.

And for the first time in his life, the guy just might be right.

42.

STAN STOMPS OVER TO THE COUNTER, HIS
eyes glued to me.

"What's going on here?" he demands as soon as he's
close enough to snatch my collar should I try and make
a run for it.

"GREE-tings, Boss," Klaus answers. "CURR-ent-*lee* I
am MAK-ing my FIRST *saaale*."

Stan takes a look at what I'm buying. And then his
eyes are right back on me, more suspicious than ever.
Probably because I'm twelve years old and out shopping for a pocket thesaurus on a snow day. Clearly he
doesn't know the kind of kids I usually hang out with.

Before the guy calls the cops or snatches up his
pickle umbrella and chases me out of the store with it,
I change the subject.

"Cool, uh, robot," I say, jerking my chin in Klaus's
direction.

"Who sent you?!" Stan barks.

I take a step back, my heart rate rising.

"It was Glen, wasn't it?"

"Glen?" I say. "I don't know any—"

"Don't you play dumb with me!" Stan snaps. "*Glen*. Owner of Glen's Bags & Rags. That punk's always had it out for me. I knew he'd get wind of my new employee here sooner or later, and that he wouldn't waste any time trying to steal him away. You just tell him that the bot works for *me*." Stan stabs a finger into his chest. "*I'm* the one who found him. It was *my* Dumpster he was digging around in. And *I'm* the one who's been spending an arm and a leg keeping him fed."

"OH yes," says Klaus. "That re-MINDS *meee*. Were you COM-ing to GET my LUNCH or-der, Boss?"

Stan whips his head toward the bot.

"Lunch?!" he cries. "It's not lunchtime yet. I only just got back from bringing you breakfast! You can't be hungry already."

"I am HUN-gry al-READ-y. It is HARD work STOCK-ing *shelves*, SWEEP-ing *floors*, TAK-ing CARE of cus-TOM-ers."

"What customers?" Stan says. He flicks his fingers toward me. "You just said this was your first one."

Klaus's eyes begin to glow a fierce and fiery red.

"FEED KLAUS LUNCH BOSS TIME FOR LUNCH FEED KLAUS OR ELSE KLAUS—"

"Okay, okay," says Stan, stopping the bot before he fries a circuit—or fires a food-cube.

Which, judging by the collection of small square holes in the wall behind him, he's done more than once before.

"You want the usual?" Stan asks the bot.

"Yes. I WOULD like the USE-u-AL. Six MEAT-ball subs, EX-tra MEAT. Nine OR-ders of *cheese* fries, EX-tra *cheese*. Two PIZZ-as with ev-er-Y-thing ON them, EX-tra ev-er-Y-thing. And LAST of all, one small SAL-ad, DRESS-ing on the *siiide*."

"Got it," Stan says.

But he doesn't go to get the bot his meal.

He goes right back to glaring at me.

I know he's not going anywhere until I make my purchase and leave his store.

So I slide my wallet out of my pocket and set a five on the counter. Klaus stabs it with a claw and deposits it in the cash register, then pokes around the drawer for my change. He holds it out to me—a pair of dollar bills shish-kebabbed on one claw and a couple of quarters pinched between the other.

"Here is YOUR change," Klaus says. "Have a SPLEN . . . SPLEN . . . SPLEN-did *daaay*."

I take my money.

Grab my thesaurus.

And go.

I've got some serious work to do.

43.

I HURRY HOME AS FAST AS I CAN, KITTY
galloping beside me, his new very, very dirty sock flapping out of his mouth like a victory flag.

We barrel through the door and into the kitchen.

There's a puddle on the floor where Edsley was standing before, plus some waffle crumbs and a splatter of syrup. But no Mike.

I lunge for the phone and, not even thinking about it, I punch in Dan's number.

Yes—I know we left things on a pretty tense note last night. And nothing has really been the same between us ever since he accidentally unleashed a horde of endlessly hungry, dangerously flatulent robots on our unsuspecting town. But now we can put all that behind us. Together, we can get rid of Klaus, and then everything can go back to how it used to be. To how it's *supposed* to be. And I don't even care if Dan really, truly does want to spend our time together talking about the vastness of the universe and the possibility that aliens might exist. Whatever. As long as we're *together*, and things aren't so flipping *weird*. Right now, that's all that matters to me.

But none of the above can happen if Dan doesn't answer the phone.

Which he's not.

The thing rings and rings and rings—and then, half a second before the call gets sent over to voice mail, someone finally picks up.

"Dan," I say, "you're never gonna believe it, man, but I—"

"Hey. *Nerd* engine. It's not your boyfriend."

It's Derek, Dan's older brother.

"Danny boy's not here," he says.

My thoughts, which have been zipping around at the speed of light, screech to a halt.

"Where is he?" I ask.

"*I* don't know," Derek says. "Out."

My thoughts start up again, but move now in a different—and significantly less pleasant—direction.

"He was here for a while with some girl," Derek continues, "but then they left. I've never seen her before. But Ken—she was, like, seriously wacky. And I'm not just saying that 'cause she was hanging out with my brother. You should've seen her. And *heard* her. She showed up with this big suitcase, and she wouldn't stop talking about *aliens*. Like, UFOs and all that. And she kept saying they were gonna make history. And I was all, What, you gonna break the world record for dorkiness? You gonna start your own country and name yourselves King and Queen of the Dweebs?"

Derek pauses for a second, probably to give me a chance to appreciate his oh-so-funny jokes.

"Ken?"

I don't answer.

"Aww, Kenny Ken," Derek chuckles. "Did I just bweak your widdle heart?"

44.

I HANG UP WITH DEREK AND RIGHT AWAY DIAL

the phone number of the next one of the guys I think of.

That guy happens to be John Henry Knox, and over at his house, several people answer the phone at once. It's John Henry's little sisters, all five or six of them—I can never remember how many there are. But the way they're giggling and shrieking in my ear, there may as well be five or six *hundred* of them.

"HELLO?!" I shout through the noise.

There's a barrage of laughs and screams, after which one of the girls shrieks, "It's a boy!"

I cling to that string of sensible sounds like it's a life preserver and I'm adrift in a violent, churning sea.

"YES!" I say. "I'm a BOY! And I REALLY NEED TO TALK TO YOUR BROTHER!"

Shriek.

Giggle.

Shriek.

And then, at last, a couple more words:

"You can't!"

Giggle.

Shriek.

Giggle.

"WHY NOT?!"

Shriek.

Shriek.

Giggle.

Shriek.

"He's not here!"

"He's out!"

"He's with a GIRL!"

SHRIEK.

GIGGLE.

GIGGLE.

GIGGLE.

SHRIEK.

My ears are ringing, but the girls are still loud enough for me to hear them start to sing:

"John and Mikaela sittin' in a tree! K-I-S-S-I-N-G! First comes love, then comes—"

I hang up.

But two seconds later, I'm dialing again.

45.

I CALL JERRY.

His mom picks up, and after making sure I've fully recovered from last night's fake sickness, she tells me the same thing the Knox girls did—though in a much more gentle, non-headache-inducing way.

"He went out with Dan and John Henry. And a girl. Michelle? Mickey? Mikaela? That's it—I'm pretty sure her name was Mikaela."

Next up is Max.

It's his dad who answers, and as soon as he finds out that it's me calling, he says, "Isn't he with you? A bunch of the guys came over to get him. I guess I just assumed you were with them too."

Then I call Alan, and Amir, and Simon, and Chris, and Rob.

I get the same story every time.

All my friends are hanging out somewhere together, and I didn't get an invite.

Probably because I made it abundantly clear that I wasn't interested in doing any of what they've been interested in doing lately.

Oops.

46.

I STAND THERE IN THE KITCHEN FOR SEVERAL

minutes, just staring at the phone and feeling sorry for myself.

I've never felt so alone.

But I'm not.

A loud, booming laugh informs me of that.

I follow the noise into the living room, and there I find Edsley.

He's lounging on the couch in my favorite hoodie and my coziest pajama pants, watching some sort of game show on TV. He's got a box of cereal on his left, a carton of milk on his right, and a blanket of crumbs covering his lap.

He glances over at me.

"Hey, man," he says. Then he turns back to the TV. "What's up?"

"I found the robot," I tell him.

"Nice," he says, cramming a handful of cereal in his

mouth, giving the clusters and flakes a few chews, then drowning it all with a couple glugs of milk.

Obviously, he's not listening to me.

I go over to the TV and hit the power button.

"Dude!" Edsley says. "I was watching that!"

"I FOUND," I tell him, nice and loud, "THE ROBOT."

Edsley's eyes go wide.

"*The* robot?" he says. "You mean the one—"

"The one that you refused to make a sandwich and then let walk right out of your house and that I've subsequently spent the majority of my saved-up allowance and essentially all of my waking hours looking for ever since, yes," I say.

Edsley blinks.

"Now come help me figure out what to do about it," I add, heading back into the kitchen.

Edsley grabs the cereal and milk and follows me there.

47.

EDSLEY AND I MAKE A PLAN.

It's by no means a brilliant one.

But it's definitely better than Edsley's first idea, which was to crawl into Things & Stuff's ductwork, remove a panel from the ceiling, and spit down at Klaus until the bot goes *SQUAH-POOM!*

Before we head out to put our plan into action, I gather some supplies:

A pair of walkie-talkies.

An ice cream scoop.

And a soup ladle.

The latter is made of some type of rubbery plastic— meaning it's flexible.

It's like a one-piece, ready-made catapult.

"Edsley?" I call once I'm all set.

He steps out of the pantry.

And it looks like he's been gathering supplies too.

He's got a box of mini donuts.

Several containers of yogurt.

And a jumbo bag of trail mix.

"Really?" I ask him.

"You said we might be out there all day."

I take a breath, and then nod.

A full Edsley is much easier to work with than a hungry one—not that working with Edsley is ever really *easy*.

Thinking this, I grab a few pieces of fruit from the bowl on the counter and stuff them in my pockets, just in case.

48.

I BRING EDSLEY TO THINGS & STUFF. THEN

lead him around back.

The snow has already begun to melt, but on the opposite side of the parking lot from the Dumpster, there's a bank of the stuff the height and width of a plow truck's blade.

It's as good a hiding spot as we're going to get.

I set Edsley up behind the snowbank, then point to the unmarked metal door off to the Dumpster's side—Things & Stuff's rear exit.

"Keep an eye on that door," I tell Edsley, handing over one of the walkie-talkies I brought. "If Klaus comes out, call me on this. Do *not* engage him in any way." I remember what Dan told me the night before—one of the things he told me, at least. "We can't risk antagonizing the guy. Okay?"

Edsley brings the walkie-talkie to his lips.

"Ten-four," he says, his voice crackling out of the

other walkie-talkie, which I've got clipped to my hip.

I start off.

My walkie-talkie crackles again.

"I forgot to say 'over,'" Edsley says. Then, a second later, he says it again: "Over."

I turn around, since I've only taken two steps.

"Mike. You don't have to say 'over.'"

He answers into his walkie-talkie.

"But how will you know when I'm done talking?" he says. "Over."

Sometimes, you have to pick your battles.

"Okay," I tell him. "You can say 'over.'"

"Good call," he says. "Over."

49.

THERE'S A BENCH MORE OR LESS RIGHT

across the street from Things & Stuff, and that's where I set myself up.

It's close enough to the store that I won't miss it if Klaus comes out, but far enough away that I won't look suspicious.

Or *too* suspicious, I should probably say.

After all, I'm a twelve-year-old kid who woke up this morning to news of a miraculous snow day, and here I am sitting on a bench holding an ice cream scoop and a soup ladle.

My walkie-talkie crackles.

I clutch the scoop and ladle more tightly, instantly on high alert.

But Edsley doesn't say anything.

He's just breathing into his walkie-talkie.

Or, I realize after listening a second longer, *chewing*.

I set down the scoop and ladle and grab my walkie-talkie just as Edsley asks, "What kind of nuts are in this trail mix? Over."

"You're supposed to be watching the door, Mike," I say.

He doesn't answer.

"Mike?"

"You didn't say 'over.' Over."

"You're supposed. To be watching. The door. *Over.*"

"I am," he says. "I can do two things at once, you know. Over."

I listen to him chew some more, trying to keep my frustration from flaring up into anger.

"Hey," he says. "What do you think everyone else is doing? Over."

I'm not expecting the question, and it throws me for a bit of a loop. All of a sudden I'm feeling a lot more than just frustrated.

Everyone else is, of course, the rest of the EngiNerds.

The guys who, if anything about the last week had been even approximately normal, we'd be with right now too.

But we're a long way from normal.

And I really don't want to talk about it right now.

Picking apart how I feel about everything that's

happened, figuring out how to get things back to normal, or even just normal*ish*—it seems like an overwhelmingly daunting task. Like trying to build a rocket ship from scratch.

So I tell Edsley, "I don't know."

And I'm hoping the conversation will end there.

It doesn't.

"They're probably sledding," Edsley says. "Over."

I keep quiet.

"Or maybe they're building a snow fort. Over."

I don't answer.

"Whatever they're doing, I bet they're doing it with that Mikaela girl. Over."

My body tenses at the sound of her name.

"Hey," Edsley says. "I've been meaning to ask . . . what do you think of her? Over."

"What do I think of her? Nothing," I say, using the same tactic I use with my parents when *they* ask me a question I don't feel like answering.

But Edsley doesn't let me get away with it.

"What do you mean, nothing?" he presses, not even waiting for me to say *over* first. "You can't think *nothing* about someone. That's, like, impossible. Even if it's just 'meh,' you've got to think *something*. Over."

◼ 138 ◼

"Okay, then. That's what I think of her. *Meh*. Over."

Edsley's silent, like he's thinking. Which usually means something stupid or gross—or stupid *and* gross—is on its way.

But Edsley's just full of surprises today.

"At first," he finally says, "I felt sort of threatened by her. But then I realized that was actually just me being impressed."

"Impressed?"

"Yeah. Not by the stuff she was talking about, really. The alien activity or whatever. But by *how* she was talking about it, I guess. She's really . . . proud. Like those T-shirts. She lets the whole world know, right up front, that she believes in something pretty much everyone else on the planet *doesn't*. That takes guts, man. It's cool. *Really* cool. I don't think I could do it. Over."

I look down at my own T-shirt. It's blue. That's it. Just blue.

"No, wait," Edsley crackles back at me. "I *know* I couldn't do it. Over."

"Mike . . . ," I say, fighting off all the confusing feelings that, thanks to him, are now swirling around inside of me. "The batteries. We can't have them dying on us. From now on, essential talk only. Got it? Over."

He doesn't answer.

Which is a relief.

I feel the tension seep out of me.

Some of it, anyway.

I spend the next few minutes trying to focus on Klaus and not Mikaela and Dan and the rest of the EngiNerds, all while hyperaware of the T-shirts that the people driving and walking by are wearing.

And then my walkie-talkie crackles again.

"Ken . . . ?" I hear.

I bring the thing back up to my mouth, ready to remind Edsley about the batteries, to tell him—

My train of thought hops the tracks.

Because something isn't sitting right.

Edsley never said *over*.

"Ken?" he says again.

And this time I hear the fear in his voice.

"Ken . . . you'd better come here."

50.

I GRAB MY SCOOP AND LADLE AND RACE

across the street.

I find Edsley precisely where I told him he *shouldn't* be. Not safely tucked out of sight behind the snowbank, but standing in the middle of the parking lot, right out in the open and just a handful of feet from Klaus, who's over by the Dumpster with a trash bag dangling from each claw.

I'm just in time to see Klaus's eyes flash red, and then hear him greet Edsley.

"Hel-lo, MICH-ael."

The words come out as flat as ever. But still, I can sense the anger behind them.

It's not exactly a warm and cuddly reunion.

"Have you COME to a-POL-o-GIZE?" the bot asks.

"Apologize?" Edsley says. "To *you*?"

I watch the fear drain right out of him, and see it replaced by a righteous anger of his own.

"*You're* the one who tried to claw my face off," Edsley says, jabbing a finger in the bot's direction.

"THAT was for CROSS-ing *meee*," Klaus argues. "You re-FUSED to MAKE me a SEC-ond SAND-wich."

"Well, *maybe*," Edsley says, "that's because you didn't show me any appreciation for the *first*."

"Do you WANT me to SHOW you some ap-PRE-ci-A-tion?" the bot asks.

"Yeah," Edsley says, lifting his chin. "I *do*."

Klaus turns his back on Edsley.

And then a small panel in the upside-down trapezoid that is the robot's pelvis slides aside.

Uh-oh.

I've seen this before.

But Edsley hasn't.

"MIKE!" I shout. "DUCK!"

51.

EDSLEY, BEING THE AWESOME DIRECTION-

follower he is, *doesn't* duck.

But fortunately, thanks to the trash bags still hanging from the bot's claws, Klaus's aim is off.

The food-cube that comes shooting out of his backside goes both low and wide, zipping past Edsley's ankle and skipping along the pavement, off into the distance.

I rush in before Klaus can fire again.

"Come on!" I tell Edsley, and just in case he decides not to follow *these* directions, I grab his arm and drag him across the parking lot.

I dive behind the snowbank, bringing Edsley down with me.

It's not a second too soon.

Fwoosh!

Fwoosh!

Fwoosh!

That's the sound of speeding food-cubes slamming into the snowbank.

"How is THAT for ap-PRE-ci-A-tion, MICH-ael?"

And *that's* the sound of a seriously ticked-off bot.

52.

A SECOND AFTER KLAUS BURIES THE FOOD-
cubes in the snowbank, we hear another sound:

SQUELCH!

The cubes react to water, the compressed comestibles expanding as soon they encounter a single drop of the stuff.

Meaning all of a sudden there are hunks of meatball subs, squashed slices of pizza, and handfuls of no-longer-hot-and-gooey cheese fries embedded in the snowbank.

It's another thing that I've seen before, but Edsley hasn't.

And he's just as amazed as I was the first time I saw a whole bunch of food seemingly appear out of nowhere.

"DUDE!" he says. "DID YOU JUST—HOW DID THAT—OH MY—"

Fwoosh!

Fwoo-fwoo-fwoo-fwoo-fwoosh!

"Not now, Mike!" I say, hoping he'll remember there's a robot over on the other side of the parking lot who's currently trying to fart him into oblivion.

SQUELCH!

SQU-SQU-SQUELCH!

Whole sausages sprout out of the snowbank.

Several turkey legs, too.

Plus enough bacon to feed a family of fifty-seven or so.

Edsley loses his mind.

"AHHH! KEN! ARE YOU SEEING THIS, MAN?!"

He plucks a piece of bacon from the snow, gives it a quick sniff, and snaps a bite off between his teeth.

I grab my ice cream scoop and drag it through the snow. Turning it over, slapping it down into my palm, I'm left holding a perfectly spherical snowball.

I set it in the shallow bowl of the soup ladle, pull back the long arm—and send the ball of densely packed flakes sailing into the side of Edsley's head.

"OW!"

He turns to me, rubbing the red spot on his temple.

"What was *that* for?"

"Focus, Mike," I tell him.

And just then, Klaus fires off another couple rounds.

Fwoo-fwoosh!

"Oh," says Edsley. "Right."

He holds out a hand.

I drop the ice cream scoop into it.

He looks me in the eye and says, "Let's turn this bot into a pile of spare parts."

53.

I STAND UP FROM BEHIND THE SNOWBANK-

and have to duck right back down again.

Fwoosh!

A food-cube zooms over my head.

"Whoa," Edsley says. He holds up a hand, the tips of his thumb and pointer finger just a smidge apart. "That was *this* close."

This was *not* the plan.

The plan was to catch Klaus off guard—to do a sneak attack, bombarding the bot with snowballs until enough moisture worked its way into his stomach to make him go *SQUAH-POOM!*

I figured it'd take five, maybe six good shots.

And I figured I could get those five or six shots off without a problem—so long as we had the element of surprise.

But that, obviously, is long gone.

"What do we do now?" Edsley asks me.

I take back the ice cream scoop and make myself a snowball.

Then I toss it up into the air.

Fwoosh!

Klaus nails the thing, instantly turning it back into flakes.

They drift down and cover the top of my head.

"What we *do*," I tell Edsley, "is make sure we get out of here alive."

He gulps.

"And how do we—" he starts.

But I don't let him finish. Instead I give him a good hard shove, sending him tumbling backwards and out from behind the snowbank.

I get to my feet just in time to see Klaus spot Edsley and adjust his body so his backside is aimed his way.

And before the bot can fire a food-cube, I chuck the ice cream scoop.

It cartwheels through the air and—

CLANG!

—smacks Klaus in the back of the head.

The robot staggers—but quickly regains his balance. At which point he whips around and fixes his flashing red eyes on me.

"FIRST cus-TOM-er?" he says. And if I could sense anger in his voice before, now I can sense *betrayal*.

I hurry over to Edsley and pull him up onto his feet.

"RUN!" I tell him, and fortunately, this is one direction he actually follows.

I risk a look back at the corner and see Klaus, his eyes still flashing, shake a razor-sharp claw over his head.

"AND DON'T COME *BAAACK*!"

54.

"MAYBE I SHOULD'VE JUST MADE THE GUY another sandwich."

It's back at my house that Edsley has this epiphany.

Unfortunately, it's six days too late.

So I ignore him and get back to doing what we've been doing ever since we returned from our run-in with the bot—figuring out how to prevent the guy from firing any food-cubes he's got left inside of him at anyone *else*.

Because if one of those things had sliced through the snowbank and hit Edsley?

Not the end of the world.

Honestly, he kind of would've *deserved* it.

But what if some little kid ventures into Things & Stuff with a bag of pretzels, and Klaus just so happens to be feeling a bit peckish? Or what if someone wanders by chewing a hunk of beef jerky the *next* time the bot goes to take out the trash?

Things could go from *bad* to *dire* in about point-zero-six seconds.

Because maybe, as long as he was working at Things & Stuff and being regularly fed by Stan, Klaus didn't pose a threat to the community. But now that he's been reunited with Edsley? Now that we've thoroughly antagonized him? We need to put the bot's butt-blasting days to an end before any of the nightmares I've been having all week come true.

Over the course of the day, Edsley and I come up with dozens of ideas about how to do this.

Most are bad.

Some are *really* bad.

And some . . .

Well, let's just say that some of them make my fan-and-chicken plan from earlier in the week seem positively brilliant.

More than once, I consider calling Dan again. I even get the urge to call up John Henry Knox. Because Edsley and I could use some help. But I'm not sure if I can take hearing from the guys' siblings and parents that they're still out who knows where doing who knows what with Mikaela. I'm also not sure what to do about Mikaela herself, and I know if I ever want to talk to the rest of the

EngiNerds again, I'm going to have to do *something*. I mean, I was wrong about her. At least a little bit. And maybe I shouldn't have been so quick to write her off. And maybe I shouldn't have *told* her off so rudely. By chasing her out of our meeting room, I thought I was protecting the EngiNerds. But that was just me being paranoid. Like Stan, "protecting" his store from any potential customer who isn't old enough to vote.

Ugh.

The thought of me being even slightly Stan-like turns my stomach.

I shove the whole distressing mess of thoughts out of my head for the time being, and refocus on the problem at hand. And finally, after talking through another handful of horrible ideas, Edsley and I come up with a plan that, with a little luck, just might work.

By the time we hammer out all the details, it's nearly seven o'clock.

Edsley calls his parents to make sure it's okay he sleeps over, then we eat a quick dinner and get right back to work.

First we slip into my dad's closet and borrow an ugly plaid suit jacket that I'm pretty sure I've never seen him wear.

Then we climb up to the attic, where we dig through a box of my old Halloween costumes.

Fifteen minutes later, we climb back down with a bowler hat, a fake mustache, a pair of lensless glasses, and a tall, crooked wizard's staff.

Done gathering what I need for my disguise, Edsley and I sit down at the computer.

It takes us the rest of the night, but when I eventually hit the print button, I'm satisfied with what we've got:

TODAY ONLY!!!

THE WORLD FAMOUS

CAN'T MISS

MUST-ATTEND

TOTALLY AWESOME

EPICALLY EXCELLENT

FESTIVAL OF COMESTIBLES!!!

FEATURING:

BOATLOADS OF BEEF

HEAPS OF HAM

STACKS OF SAUSAGE

IMPOSSIBLE QUANTITIES OF PORK

TOO MUCH TUNA

AND

DEFINITELY NO RADISHES!

TODAY! 10:00 AM! FELDMAN'S FIELD!

ROBOTS WELCOME!

BE THERE OR BE HUNGRY!

I based the fake festival's food offerings on what had *SQUELCH*ed into being in the snowbank behind Things & Stuff. And it was Edsley who suggested the made-up event should be held at Feldman's Field. The place is old and overgrown. No one goes there anymore to play kickball or run around. We'll have it all to ourselves.

Which is just how I want it when we finally make Mr. How Is That for Appreciation go *SQUAH-POOM!*

55.

THAT NIGHT, FORTUNATELY, THERE ARE NO
farting robots or talking clouds waiting for me in my
dreams.

*Un*fortunately, that's mostly because I barely sleep
a wink, and don't even really get a chance to *have* a
dream.

Why?

I'm nervous, for one thing.

All right—I'm *scared*.

Scared that our plan isn't going to work.

Scared that it's only going to further antagonize
Klaus—and maybe antagonize him so much that he
decides to rampage around town, butt-blasting the
place to bits.

But the other, bigger reason I don't get much sleep?

Edsley.

He spends half the night snoring like a brontosaurus
with a severe sinus infection.

The other half of the night he spends talking in his sleep, giving me a bizarre and frankly pretty uncomfortable peek into *his* dreams.

"Not the mango!" he says at one point.

Then, later:

"Thank you for the invitation, Mr. Fuzzy Rump!"

And not too long after that:

"Pony, pony, pony, pony, pony, pony, pony!"

This last outburst is loud enough to wake up my dad. He pokes his head into my bedroom, all bleary-eyed, to make sure everything is okay.

I tell him yes, and he leaves, and then I smack Mike in the face with a pillow.

This stops him from shouting out random gibberish—but then he just goes right back to snoring.

By that point, the sun's already coming up, and I figure I might as well just start my day.

I get out of bed and head down to the kitchen, where Edsley's snores aren't quite as thunderous as a brontosaurus's—I'd say they're more like a stegosaurus's.

It's Saturday, and I usually spend Saturday mornings visiting my grandpa.

I can't today, obviously. I've got a date with a robot.

So I call up Grandpa K. to let him know.

One thing you should probably know about my grandpa: He doesn't talk. Not how people normally talk, at least. He doesn't use words. But I understand him all the same. Even over the phone, as long as I'm listening closely, everything he's trying to tell me comes through loud and clear.

The old man picks up after just one ring.

"Grandpa?" I say. "It's Ken. I just wanted to let you know that I can't come over today with Dad. I'm, ah . . . busy."

On the other end of the line, Grandpa clucks his tongue.

"I know," I say. "Maybe I can come by tomorrow. Or during the week."

Grandpa sucks his teeth, then gives a little whistle.

"Things?" I say. "Things are . . . good."

I hear a series of soft clicks. I know what it is—Grandpa passing a toothpick from one side of his mouth to the other. The clicks are the thin stick of wood tapping against the tops and bottoms of his teeth.

After listening for a moment, I blow the air out of my cheeks.

"Okay," I say. "Maybe things aren't *good*. I guess you could say they're . . . *weird*."

Grandpa clucks his tongue again, then sniffs.

I try to think of a way to say what I have to say that doesn't make me sound like a *totally* terrible person.

"I was wrong about someone. Maybe even really wrong. Because I was stressed out. And scared. And confused. And—and *stubborn*. And I guess, because of all that, I . . . well, I was kind of a jerk."

It feels surprisingly good to say it out loud.

"Or not *kind of*," I clarify. "I was *definitely* a jerk."

That feels even better.

Grandpa gives me another sniff. Then I hear the *click-clickety-click* of his toothpick. Finally, he grunts.

"I know," I tell him. "You're right. I have to apologize. And then I have to prove that I'm *not* actually a stubborn jerk."

Grandpa takes a deep, contented breath.

"Don't worry," I say. "I'm gonna do exactly that. First I've just got to keep something from biting me and my friends in the backside."

56.

I GET OFF THE PHONE WITH GRANDPA AND

head back upstairs.

Edsley's still asleep.

I let him snore while I get on my disguise.

All dressed in my hat, glasses, and suit jacket, the fake mustache firmly pressed to the flesh above my lip, I nudge Edsley awake with the butt of my wizard's staff.

"Pony!" he shouts, his eyes suddenly as big as dinner plates.

He stares at me.

Blinks.

Shakes his head.

"How do I look?" I ask him.

He yawns as he gives me a once-over.

"You look," he says, "like a really short wizard who's trying to pass himself off as a guy from the nineteenth century."

I open my mouth.

"Or no," Edsley says before I can get a word out. "You look like a really short guy from the nineteenth century who fell and hit his head and so now he *thinks* he's a wizard."

I sigh.

"No wait. You look like—"

"*Mike*," I interrupt. "All that matters is that Klaus doesn't recognize me from yesterday."

"Well," Edsley says, looking me over again, "as long as he doesn't know any really short wizards from the nineteenth century who have absolutely zero fashion sense, I don't think he'll recognize you at all."

I grab the Festival of Comestibles flier and tell Edsley to meet me downstairs.

There, I fill up my backpack with as much portable liquid as I can find:

Six bottles of water.

A couple of juice boxes.

Two cans of ginger ale.

And a quarter-carton of milk.

Edsley steps into the kitchen just as I'm rearranging things in the bag to fit the milk.

"What about all this stuff?" he says, setting a hand on one of the shelves of the refrigerator door.

There's a jar of apple sauce.

A jar of strawberry jam.

A squeeze bottle of ketchup.

A squeeze bottle of mustard.

And a squeeze bottle of chocolate syrup.

I add it all to my backpack, just in case.

Then I hand the bag to Edsley.

He slings it over his shoulder and heads for the door.

But I hang back and take a good long look at my kitchen. Hopefully, I think, it's not the last time I see it.

57.

ON OUR WAY TO THINGS & STUFF, MY mustache falls off four times.

This does nothing to help my stress levels, which are already sky-high.

Just outside the store, the mustache falls off *again*.

This time, Edsley picks it up for me. And then, before I can ask him what in the heck he thinks he's doing, he drags the back of the 'stache over his tongue and slaps it onto my face.

"That should do it," he says.

I gag like I do at the dentist when they jam those sharp little X-ray pads down your throat. And it's a good thing I skipped breakfast, otherwise it'd probably be making a reappearance right about now.

Doing my best to ignore the fact that Edsley basically just licked my face, I turn to Things & Stuff.

The snow that was heaped in front of the store the

day before is already nearly gone. The mid-May sun made quick work of melting it.

I take a deep breath—and Edsley claps me on the back, knocking the air back out of me.

"Go get 'em, you weird-lookin' wizard," he says.

58.

"WEL-COME TO THINGS AND STUFF. HOW MAY
I HA . . . HA . . . HELP *youuu?*"

Klaus is at the back of the store, a feather duster pinched in one claw and a wet cloth dangling from the other.

I waggle my wizard's staff in greeting, then lower my head and mutter something about how I'm just browsing.

But the bot seems even more excited than he was the day before about having a real live customer in the store. He abandons his cleaning equipment and makes his way over, bringing a little cloud of dust along with him. The tiny particles crowd my face, making my eyes itch and my nose tickle.

"You ARE an in-TER-est-ing LOOK-ing cus-TOM-er," Klaus says, now so close to me that, if robots had breath, I'd be able to smell his. "You ARE my SEC-ond cus-TOM-er. My FIRST cus-TOM-er turned OUT to be a NIN-com-*poop.*"

A *nincompoop*? Really?

Making my voice as gruff as possible, I say, "Oh, well, I'm sure he was a fine person."

"NO," Klaus says. "TOE-tal NIN-com-*poop*."

A part of me wants to continue to defend myself. But a larger part of me just wants to hurry up and get out of there.

So I dig a hand into the pocket of my dad's suit jacket, which is where I stashed the Festival of Comestibles flier. I pull it out—and then let it slip through my fingers and fall to the floor.

"HERE," says Klaus, spotting the piece of paper. "All-OW me to GET that for *youuu*."

The bot bends over, shifting the dust that's still hanging around us so that another puff of the stuff hits my nose. I try to twitch the tickle out of it while I watch Klaus spear the flier on a claw. Standing back up, he holds it out to me—but then, before I can even reach for it, he tugs it back.

His eyes lock on the text, and then begin to flicker.

"BOAT-loads of *beeef*?" he says.

"Oh yes," I tell him in my gruff voice. "The Festival of Comestibles. Today only. Starts very soon."

The little light bulb on top of Klaus's head is burning so brightly, I'm afraid the thing's going to burst.

"Ro-bots are WEL-come?" he asks.

"Of course," I say. "You just have to be at Feldman's Field at ten o'clock."

"Feld-man's FIELD," Klaus states. "Al-so KNOWN as lo-CAY-shun   one-NINE-four-NINE-two-NINE-NINE-NINE-NINE-NINE-NINE-NINE-NINE-NINE-NINE-NINE-six-NINE."

I nod, dipping my nose right back into the dust.

"That sounds—*ahh*-CHOO!"

I sneeze hard enough to knock my mustache loose.

It flies toward the floor and hits it with a soft wet *slap*.

With my heart suddenly hammering hard enough to crack right through my ribs, I clap a hand over my mouth and wait for the worst to happen—for Klaus to identify me as the "nincompoop" from the day before, and for him to then turn around and hit me with a turd-missile at close range.

But several, fart-less seconds tick by.

I look up—and see that Klaus hasn't even taken his flickering eyes off the flier.

Quickly, I shove the 'stache under the nearest shelf with the end of my wizard's staff. Then I say, "See you there!" and head for the door.

I don't stick around to find out if Klaus replies.

I'm gone—outside to collect Edsley, and then on to Feldman's Field, where we'll wait and hope.

Hope that the robot really does show up.

And hope that we've got what it takes to handle him.

59.

IT TAKES FIFTEEN MINUTES TO WALK FROM
Things & Stuff to Feldman's Field.

Edsley and I make it in ten.

I chalk my own speed-walking up to nervousness.

And though Edsley keeps having to break into a jog
to keep up with me, I can tell he's nervous too.

The whole walk, he doesn't say a single word.

He also doesn't sneak into the backpack to have
some of the ginger ale or chocolate syrup we brought
with us.

And when we pass by Cheese Louise's, he doesn't
tip his head back and get a whiff of the cheese and
grease. He doesn't even glance at the inviting pictures
of crispy fries and gooey, pepperoni-packed slices plas-
tered to the pizza shop's windows.

It turns out we're right to be nervous.

Because before we even step out onto Feldman's
Field, something goes wrong.

The field—the old, overgrown patch of grass that no one ever goes to anymore—isn't empty.

There are a bunch of kids on it, all standing in a cluster just past a set of old rusty bleachers.

I head their way, already wondering how in the world I'm going to chase them off in the next sixty seconds.

But these thoughts dissolve as soon as I get a little closer.

The first one of the kids I recognize is Max.

And then Amir.

Then Simon.

Alan.

Jerry.

Chris.

Rob.

John Henry Knox.

Dan.

It's all of them—every single one of the other EngiNerds.

Plus, of course, Mikaela.

60.

WHAT ARE ALL THE GUYS—AND MIKAELA—

doing here?

Could they have somehow heard about the Festival of Comestibles?

Did Edsley tell them?

"Mike?"

It's Dan.

He eyes Edsley, then turns to me, still carrying the wizard's staff and wearing a bowler hat, some lensless glasses, and my dad's ugly plaid suit jacket.

"Ken?" he says, squinting to make sure. "What's going on?"

Before I can turn the question around on him, his eyes go wide.

Then everyone else's do too.

They're all focused on something over my shoulder.

And even before I hear him, I know he's arrived.

"Where is THE *beeeef*?"

61.

KLAUS IS PEERING AROUND AT THE SUN-
bleached weeds and torn plastic bags and deflated soccer balls littering Feldman's Field, his neck making little clicking noises as his head swivels.

His eyes flash red.

The light bulb on his head burns brightly enough to be seen from outer space.

Finally, the bot's gaze settles on me.

"SEC-ond cus-TOM-er," he says. "I have ar-RIVED at lo-CAY-shun one-NINE-four-NINE-two-NINE-NINE-NINE-NINE-NINE-NINE-NINE-NINE-NINE-NINE-NINE-NINE-six-NINE. The FES-ti-VAL of Com-EST-ib-ulls is to BE-gin in ONE min-UTE and four-TEEN SEC-onds. Now in ONE min-UTE and TWELVE SEC-onds. I ASK *youuu*: Where is THE—"

Before the bot can finish this question, another one occurs to him:

"Where IS your MUS-tache?"

He takes a step closer to me. His eyes pulse in a new pattern.

"You ARE not SEC-ond cus-TOM-er," he says. "You ARE FIRST cus-TOM-er. You ARE NIN-com-*poop*."

Click-click-click.

Klaus turns his head like he's looking for something.

Or some*one*.

His gaze lands on Edsley.

"MICH-ael," he says. "I SHOULD have *knooown*."

Click-click-click—the bot's eyes refocus on me.

"There IS no FES-ti-VAL of Com-EST-ib-ulls. There IS no *beeeef*."

Klaus points one razor-sharp claw at me.

The other he aims at Edsley.

"CROSS me once," he says, "shame ON *youuu*. CROSS me twice . . ." The bot does an about-face and pokes his butt in my direction. ". . . I FART ON *YOUUU*."

62.

I STAND THERE AND WATCH THE SMALL PANEL

in the upside-down trapezoid that is the robot's pelvis slide aside.

Of course I know what's coming next.

And I know that I need to get out of there—*fast*.

But I can't get myself to move.

Because it wasn't supposed to go like this.

Edsley and I were supposed to have time to set up before Klaus arrived.

The rest of the EngiNerds weren't supposed to be here.

And Mikaela wasn't either.

But thank God she is.

Because before the bot can send a food-cube speeding my way, Mikaela charges forward.

She snatches the wizard's staff out of my hand and, winding up as she races toward the bot, swings the thing into the guy's back.

Ka-CLA-yAng-ang-ang-ang!

Klaus tips forward, stiff as a tree trunk, and face-plants onto the ground with a satisfying *THUD*.

And then:

Pew!

The food-cube that was meant for me goes rocketing up into the air.

I find Mikaela's eyes.

But what do you say to the person who just saved you from a potentially fatal robot fart?

I don't think they make a greeting card for that.

Not to mention the fact that there's a whole bunch of *other* stuff I need to say to Mikaela. Like sorry for being a huge stubborn jerk for the past few days, and also thanks for giving me the data-eater even though I didn't want it, since the thing was kinda sorta the reason why I finally found Klaus.

"Um," I say. "Tha—"

I don't even get the whole word out.

A faint whistling from above interrupts me.

Mikaela realizes what it is before I do, and suddenly she's charging forward *again*.

She yanks me out of the way just before the food-cube that Klaus sent soaring into the sky comes shrieking back down—and lands in the *exact* spot where I was standing.

It makes a little crater in the earth.

Turning back to Mikaela, I try again.

"Tha—"

"No time!" she shouts, pointing at Klaus, who's already climbing back to his feet, and then grabbing hold of my arm and yanking me once more—this time across the field toward those old rusty bleachers, which I now see the rest of the EngiNerds have upended and barricaded themselves behind.

63.

KLAUS IS HUNGRY.

And angry.

He's capital-h *Hangry*.

"Where is THE *beeeef*?" he demands.

Then—

Pew! Pew! Pew!

—he fires a few food-cubes our way.

Plink!

Plonk!

Plunk!

Those are the sounds the cubes make as they ricochet off the bleachers, each shot sending a spray of dark red rust up into the air.

All of us—every last EngiNerd, plus Mikaela—are huddled behind the seats, crouched low with our limbs contorted to make sure we're not the least bit exposed.

My mind is reeling.

It was hard enough to come up with *one* decent plan

for fooling and defeating the bot, and I did that in the peace and quiet of my own home. Here, now, with the Hangry, double-crossed butt-blaster at my back, I can't think of anything to do besides panic and hide.

"KEN!"

It's Dan, army crawling over to me.

And I don't know what it is—maybe the cure for a strained friendship is to risk being farted into oblivion together—but after only a couple seconds of our looking into each other's eyes, all the aggravation and anger and hurt that's been building up between us for the past week begins to melt away faster than a pint of ice cream on a record-breakingly hot day.

And then the apologies start pouring out.

"Listen," he says. "I—"

"Wait," I stop him. "I want to say—"

"No," he interrupts. "*I* want to say that I shouldn't have—"

"*I* shouldn't have—" I cut him off.

"But I—"

"But *I*—"

"If I hadn't—"

"You only—"

"HEY!"

It's Edsley, whose lying just a short ways from us.

"Maybe you two can kiss and make up later?" he says. "Now might not be the best time."

P-P-Pew!

Plink-plonk-plunk!

Dan and I don't argue.

Edsley crawls the rest of the way over to us, dragging my backpack along beside him. He shoves it toward me, and out spill all of the bottles and boxes and jars and cans we stuffed in there earlier.

"The way I see it," Edsley says, "the only way out of this mess is to use our numbers to our advantage." He jerks his thumb in the direction of the bot. "There's only one of him, but there's . . ." Edsley bends around and starts to count. " . . . one, two, three, four—" He stops. "A ton of us! There's a whole butt-ton of us!"

Dan and I exchange a look.

Then turn back to Edsley.

"Mike," I say, "that might just be the smartest thing you've ever said."

64.

DAN, EDSLEY, AND I DISTRIBUTE THE GOODS,

then tell everyone the plan. Which, technically speaking, isn't really a plan. It's more of a mission statement: Douse the bot—but *don't* get hit by one of his farts.

We make sure everyone understands and is as ready as you could ever be to enter into a ludicrously high-stakes food fight with a farting robot.

It's Mikaela who suggests, "On three?"

There are nods and thumbs-up all around.

Dan does the honors.

"One—" he begins.

And that's when Edsley, clutching the squeeze bottle of chocolate syrup, springs to his feet, darts around the overturned bleachers, and, screeching like a deranged seagull, charges toward the bot.

"MIKE!" I call after him.

Because I assume he's just being his usual, brilliant-yet-somehow-unbelievably-idiotic self, and that he's somehow failed to grasp the concept of *on three*. But then I realize I'm wrong. That Edsley has jumped the gun on purpose. That he's leading the charge, putting himself in the greatest danger so that the rest of us will have a better shot at accomplishing our goal.

Watching him sprint across the field toward Klaus, I feel all sorts of things I've never before felt for Edsley, and that I honestly never could've imagined myself feeling for him *ever*: admiration, appreciation, amazement at something besides his seemingly limitless capacity for grossness.

And when Edsley, still a handful of feet from the bot, shouts, "HOW ABOUT A LITTLE EYE CANDY, SIR FARTS-A-LOT?" which, of course, doesn't really make any sense—well, not even that can detract from the awesomeness of the moment.

Hoisting the bottle of chocolate syrup over his shoulder like a battle-ax, Edsley gives the thing a fierce squeeze, squirting the dark, goopy liquid right into the robot's eyes, coating them both and basically blinding the guy.

Dan shouts, "THREE!"

And then all the rest of us are on our feet, darting around the bleachers and charging onto the field—a whole pack of us moving together as one.

65.

CHAOS.

Bedlam.

Mayhem.

Pandemonium.

These words can be found grouped together in my Things & Stuff pocket thesaurus, but none of them quite capture the extent of the disorder and confusion that ensue once we all get out onto Feldman's Field.

Within seconds, I've got apple sauce in my eye and ginger ale up my nose.

Somehow, my hat ends up on Jerry's head.

And my glasses—don't ask me how—find their way into my shoe.

There's a lot of shouting.

And even more *pew-pew-pew*-ing.

I look around, a bottle of water clenched in one hand, searching for Klaus.

But all I can see are ducking and diving EngiNerds and flying juice boxes and jars of strawberry jam.

Pew-SQUELCH!

Suddenly my leg is soaked, and my bottle of water has been reduced to a mangled piece of plastic. On the ground nearby are a pile of chicken tenders and a hunk of barbecue sauce-slathered roast beef.

I toss aside what's left of the bottle and look in the direction of that last *pew*.

A glob of ketchup splats across my forehead—and then a brown-black blur zips through my vision.

I wipe off the ketchup and then hurry in the direction the speeding food-cube came from.

Zigzagging around a few of the guys, I finally find the bot.

He's still got chocolate syrup smeared all over his face.

But besides that, he's perfectly clean.

Somehow, he's managed to dodge every single one of our projectiles.

Not a single drop of liquid has gotten anywhere close to his food-cube-filled belly.

The ground is littered with empty bottles of water,

squashed juice boxes, crushed cans of ginger ale, splashes of milk, splatters of ketchup and mustard and apple sauce and jam.

It looks like we're all out of ammunition. . . .

And Klaus is as Hangry as ever, seething and shouting—and, of course, firing off food-cubes left and right.

"NO one CROSSES *Klaus*," he says.

Pew-pew!

Simon dives out of the way in the nick of time.

"Where is THE *beeeef*?"

Pew!

Amir leaps into the air, the food-cube sailing between his hastily spread legs.

"Where is THE *tooo*-NA?"

P-P-Pew! P-P-P-P-Pew!

Rob and Chris and Max and Alan duck and dodge and cower and crouch.

"Where is THE—"

The bot stops the instant he spots her: Mikaela.

She's not hiding, or standing around helplessly. She's striding right toward Klaus, as self-assured as ever, a small remote control with a single, round red button in her hand.

She plants her feet about a yard away from the bot, just out of clawing distance.

Then she holds up the remote.

Klaus stares down at the gadget, chocolate syrup dripping from his flashing red eyes.

"Is that FOR tel-e-VIS-ion?" he asks.

"I'm afraid not," Mikaela says. "This is something called an emergency immobilizer." She tosses the remote into the air and catches it in her opposite hand. "One push of this little red button here, and your circuits fry. Your resistors and transistors and capacitators and inductors get hopelessly overloaded and *you*, my metal friend, go up in smoke."

Klaus's eyes stop flashing and burn a bright, alarmed red.

"Per-HAPS you should NOT press the LITT-le red BUTT-on *theeere.*"

Mikaela gives the bot a grin.

Then she presses the button.

But nothing happens.

She presses it again.

Nada.

She jams her thumb down on the thing.

But it's no use.

"HA-HA-HA-*haaaa*," Klaus says. "Now I SHALL em-er-GEN-*ceee* imm-O-bull-IZE *youuu*."

The bot lunges forward and swipes a claw at Mikaela. She leaps back just in time.

"Do something!"

It's Edsley, hissing in my ear and tugging on my arm like he wants to tear the thing out of its socket.

Panicking, I scan the ground around me, hoping to find at least a sip's worth of water left in one of the bottles.

I don't.

All I see is my wizard's staff, lying a few feet away.

Edsley tugs on my arm again—

And of all things, Kitty pops into my mind.

"Mikaela!" I shout a split second after the pooch appears in my head.

She takes another couple quick steps back from Klaus, then glances over at me, at the same time shouting, "This better be good!"

I aim my eyes at her remote control, then swing them up toward the sky, and then, finally, aim them over at my wizard's staff.

And either Mikaela's just as brilliant as Dan promised me she was, or she's got a lovably dumb, endlessly gullible dog of her own at home, because she gets it right away, she knows that I'm suggesting we go for the Ol' Make Him Look.

And she doesn't waste any time doing so.

She takes one last step back and then chucks her remote control straight up into the air.

I hesitate just long enough to make sure Klaus falls for it, tipping his head back and watching the gadget spin higher and higher into the sky.

Then I snatch up the wizard's staff and run at him.

He looks back down as soon as he hears my foot-steps.

But by then it's too late.

I'm already yanking the staff back over my shoulder, then swinging, and—

CLA-yA-yA-yA-yA-yANG!

The force of the blow rides up my wrists and through my arms, making my elbows shudder.

Klaus lurches, staggers, and spins in a teetering circle.

I watch him, hoping that he'll hurry up and topple over—and that this time, he'll *stay* down.

John Henry Knox does me one better:

"GET HIM!" he cries.

The rest of the EngiNerds all rush the bot, and the

first few to make it over dive on top of him, knocking him down and pinning his limbs to the ground.

Klaus struggles against them, almost immediately slipping an arm and then a leg free from their grasp.

"QUICK!" shouts Edsley. "EVERYBODY SPIT ON HIM!"

It's as stupid an idea as it was when Mike suggested it yesterday. But in the heat of the moment, I can't think of anything better, so I purse my lips along with Mike and get ready to spray the bot with some saliva.

"WAIT!" Mikaela stops us.

She points a finger at the pile of squirming bodies and turns to the EngiNerds who aren't busy wrestling the bot.

"Get your tools!" she cries.

The guys don't hesitate.

Max hurries over with a little utility knife.

Amir produces a set of Allen wrenches.

Alan's got a screwdriver.

Simon has a pair of pliers.

And Mikaela?

She doesn't have a tool, and not another one of her fancy gadgets either. But she's got something else—

something even more important. She's got that intangible thing that's needed to get the guys working together. The thing that, no matter how hard I tried, I couldn't manage to summon all week. The glue that makes us more than the sum of our parts, that helps turn us into a team.

Not just a bunch of nerds, but the *EngiNerds*.

And if Mikaela isn't an EngiNerd—well, then I don't know who is.

Thanks to her spot-on instructions, Max, Amir, Alan, and Simon get the robot dismantled in no time. Klaus is no longer a single entity capable of walking, talking, clawing, accusing, and farting speeding food-cubes. He's a pile of parts: a head, a torso, two arms, and two legs. Last of all, just in case, Amir detaches the robot's feet and sets them in the grass beside the rest of him.

After that, we all just stand there.

Panting.

Catching our breath.

Wiping the gobs of mustard and blobs of strawberry jam off our shins and sleeves.

Finally, I'm able to ask the question that I'd been about to ask before Klaus showed up.

"What are you all doing here?"

It's John Henry Knox who answers.

"We did it," he tells me.

"Did what?" I say.

He turns to Mikaela.

She glances at the watch on her wrist.

Then she points up at the sky.

66.

I LOOK UP.

And there, dominating the sky, is a cloud.

Or not *a* cloud.

The cloud.

It's just like the one I saw the other night on my way home from Jerry's, and just like the one that appeared above my house the day my microwave went berserk, and just like the one that came to the rescue a week ago behind the Shop & Save.

Except now, it doesn't look so much like a shopping mall–size anvil made of cotton balls. It looks to me a lot more like a UFO covered in clouds.

And somehow, as big as the thing is, it's getting even *bigger*.

Or, I realize, it's just dropping down out of the sky.

Clouds don't usually do that, I know.

But this one does.

It sinks lower and lower, almost as if it's being piloted

and coming in for a landing on Feldman's Field.

Watching it, my brain begins to throb, like someone's trying to cram way too much into it.

"Guys?" I say. "Is that . . ."

I can't get myself to finish.

But that doesn't matter.

Only a moment later, the cloud settles onto the field. Its fluffy white puffs and lumps continue to billow and curl. And then a portion of the cloud, a chunk right in the center, begins to swirl a little more than any of the other parts. The white wisps thin out and turn gray-ish, and are then blown away to reveal a flat patch of something charcoal-colored. It looks metallic, and it's slightly curved, sort of like a car door.

I think this—and then the dark patch slides aside.

It *opens*.

Because it *is* a door.

And standing there in the doorway is a figure, lit from behind by a strong, bright light.

67.

YES.

That's the answer to the question you're no doubt wondering.

The figure standing in the doorway is, indeed, an extraterrestrial. An alien. A being from another planet.

A ramp emerges from a slot beneath the open doorway, then reaches for the ground like a long metallic tongue.

The alien makes his way down the ramp, revealing himself a little more with every step.

He's got two arms.

Two legs.

And a fairly human-like face.

His eyes look a bit too big.

His nose seems a tad too narrow.

And his skin has an odd, green-blue tinge to it.

But besides that, you might mistake him for a regular twelve-year-old kid.

He's even got the clothes to fit the part: a T-shirt with a cartoon skateboarder on it, a pair of baggy shorts, and some sneakers.

When he gets to the bottom of the ramp, the alien stops.

He takes a deep breath.

And then steps out onto the field.

He studies us for a moment before he speaks.

"Sorry about the blackout." His voice sounds pretty normal, though there's a high-pitched edge to it—a squeaky thread running through each word. "And the satellite." He looks right at me. "And your microwave." Turning back to everyone else, he smiles and says, "I trust the snow day made up for it?"

No one answers.

Because just now, I don't think any of us are capable of speech.

I'm pretty sure most of the guys have forgotten how to *breathe*.

After a moment, the alien moves on.

"Well, then," he says. "Surely you are all wondering what it is I am doing here."

Mikaela manages a single, small nod.

"I am here—"

Suddenly, the alien shuts his eyes.

My heart starts to beat a bit harder.

Sweat prickles up on my forehead and the back of my neck.

Is the alien's reason for being here so terrible that he can't even bear to tell us?

FFFffpffweeeeeeeeeeeeeeeeeeeeeeeee-PARP!

It sounds like someone with a too-tiny mouth trying to play a trumpet, followed by that same someone burping and popping a bubble at the same time.

The alien rests a hand on his stomach.

"Excuse me," he says, opening his eyes. "Those Food-Plus veggie burgers are *not* sitting well." He clears his throat. "Anyway, I am here to let you know that your planet is in grave danger. If something is not done, it will be reduced to dust within a week."

Beside me, Mikaela gulps.

"A . . . week?" she says.

The alien lifts a shoulder, then lets is fall.

"Two if you're lucky."

Acknowledgments

THANK YOU TO MY FAMILY AND FRIENDS FOR the love and countless other things.

Thank you to Myrsini Stephanides for the support, encouragement, and advocacy. Also for patiently explaining (and then occasionally re-explaining) all the stuff about this book-making business that I don't understand.

Thank you to Karen Nagel and Tricia Lin for the attention, care, and enthusiasm you've shown these books, in particular when you're (kindly, constructively) telling me they aren't as good as they can be and helping me make them so much better.

Thank you to Serge Seidlitz for yet another unbelievably awesome cover.

Thank you to Karin Paprocki, Beth Adelman, Hilary Zarycky, Mara Anastas, and everyone else at Simon & Schuster/Aladdin who had a hand in making this book a reality.

Thank you to every educator, librarian, bookseller, parent, and other person who has helped get my books into the hands of young readers. And thanks especially to those educators and librarians who have become such a cherished part of my book life—you know who you are, and you *should* know that you were already included in these acknowledgments when I thanked my "family and friends."

Thank you to my debut group, and all the other creators I've met on this journey so far, for the camaraderie, whether we're celebrating, commiserating, or critiquing.

And a big, huge, heartfelt THANK-YOU to my readers, every single one of the kids (and kids at heart) I've been lucky enough to meet, listen to, learn from, and share the excitement of stories and storytelling with.

And last but most of all, thank you to my two everythings: Danni and Isla.

About the Author

JARRETT LERNER KNOWS THERE'S FAR more he doesn't know than he knows. (In other words, he's pretty sure there are aliens out there, somewhere or other.) He lives with his wife, his daughter, and a cat in Medford, Massachusetts. You can visit him online at jarrettlerner.com and find him on Twitter at @Jarrett_Lerner.